PARASITIC OMENS

JESSICA A. MCMINN

Parasitic Omens

A Gods of Dallalmar Story

Jessica A. McMinn

Contents

Also By

Gardens of War & Wasteland

The Collector's Lost Things

Call of the Huntress

The Ruptured Sky

The Blood Curse

Gods of Dallalmar

Parasitic Omens

TRIGGER WARNINGS
READER DISCRETION ADVISED

Parasitic Omens is a gaslamp fantasy horror and contains the following content and trigger warnings:

Strong language

Violence

Gore

Corpse desecration

Body mutilation

Child abuse (off page)

Eldritch horror

If you are impacted by any of the above events, this may not be the book for you.

Please proceed at your own discretion.

1

PARASITE

THE WINDOW OF THE Dripping Bucket had been smashed in again and Briar was already flogging the perpetrators out back. Patrons paused to listen to the hollow thuds and groans wafting through the tavern like a bad smell. Some flinched in sympathy with each blow; others scowled in mild annoyance as they struggled to hear the bard over the ruckus; and Lawrence Reed pushed through the rabble to signal the barman for a pint.

He took off his hat, set it down on the scarred mahogany, and dropped onto a stool with his back to the bar. The evening's clientele was the usual riffraff: Copperton's rowdy working class, here to spend their week's wages on booze and breasts before the coin even hit their pockets. Law'd seen them all before, and likely would again.

Not because there was no where else to drink in this piss-hole of a town, but because Briar kept the liquor cheap and the place relatively clean—provided no one looked too hard at the old bloodstains beneath the sawdust on the floor.

'Your tab's full again, Law,' the barkeeper said, placing a watered-down beer beside Law's elbow.

'I know,' he replied without turning back to regard the man. 'I want to speak to Briar.'

'I'd like a word with you, too,' a woman replied; this time, Law swivelled on his stool.

Briar Loren wiped her hands on her apron as though she'd been out back washing glasses, not dishing out corporal punishment. A fine smattering of blood freckled the garment's frayed hem. She was a severe woman, with silver-streaked mousy hair braided and coiled atop her head like a crown. Middle-aged and unwed, the gossip was her thorny nature kept men from her bed; in truth, Briar had fallen in love years ago—with her work.

'Ms Loren,' Law greeted with a dip of his head.

'Mr Reed,' she returned flatly. 'Full tab again? Someone needs help managing his coin.'

'More like workload,' he grunted. His eyes drifted to the leather folder wedged between two bottles of whisky on the back counter—the folder that Briar stuffed with newspaper clippings and scrawled notes requesting help from investigators of the occult, the arcane, and the supernatural.

It was empty.

'Someone beat me to it?' Law scoffed, pointing his chin at the deflated file and reaching for the cigarillo case inside his coat.

'Been quiet.' Briar folded her arms and waited for the barkeeper to move further away, then leant in for Law's ears only. '*I* have a job for you, though.'

Law shifted uncomfortably on his stool, the wood harder than it had been when he first sat down. Briar Loren often had jobs that needed doing, and Law was one of the few people she trusted to get them done. Despite the help she offered investigators to rid Copperton of the strange and the unnatural, she was very much at the centre of it.

Briar Loren was an alchemist. She was acquainted with every witch, conjurer and soothsayer this side of the capital. She knew when new faces came to town and when old ones were out of line—prompting a visit from someone like Law. Some clients came to her directly; other jobs she pieced together from whispers and rumours to be handed out like rations to her network of agents. Inexperienced or arrogant investigators might try to source their own work, but anyone who'd been in Copperton long enough knew that if a job was worth pursuing, Briar Loren already had a man on it.

Law struck a match, lit his cigarillo, and waited for Briar to start talking. Her grey eyes darted around the room, drawn to the scuffle currently brewing in the tavern behind him. Law heard the rising voices, the jeers cutting above the steady strumming of the minstrel's lute. He'd thought having someone flogged already would've settled things down.

Apparently not.

'There's a body in the woods,' Briar said, the words tumbling out with her sigh.

Law watched the smoke curl off the end of his cigarillo. 'There's always a body in the woods.'

'A fresh one. Not yet buried.'

That didn't make it any more unusual. There were always bodies in the Taschenwilde—fresh, buried or otherwise. The thick, misty tangle of tree and thicket was miles wide, a veritable barricade between Copperton and Sunscourt, the regional capital and seat of the king, who didn't much care about what went on south of the forest. Even Lord Harrison, a viscount who held land within the boundaries of this stinking shit hole, held little interest in how it was governed. So long as the people paid their taxes, respected his status and otherwise left him alone, he would do the same for them.

Which is why there were so many bodies in the woods.

'Witches or warlocks?' Law asked, though he dreaded the answer. Both had a penchant for harvesting bodily sundries for their arts and dumping mangled corpses in the forest. He'd cleaned up his fair share of their waste and had thought they'd driven the *darker* practitioners from Copperton months ago.

Perhaps not.

'Fortunately, neither, but I'm out of liver. Hoping this body still has one intact.'

Briar's agents cut their teeth at a young age, sourcing work for her little empire of the occult. She'd done the work herself, once—when she was younger. Now, her rats in training did it for her. Law himself got started lurking in the back alley by the undertakers', sniffing out mysterious deaths for Briar's investigators to solve. He hadn't done *that* in a while.

Stubbing his cigarillo into a heavy glass ashtray, he said, 'Thought I was past being your errand boy.'

'You are. But as you can see, my hands are rather full here tonight.' Briar rolled her wrists, gesturing at the tavern around her. 'Harvestthe liver and I'll clear your tab. Otherwise,' and she moved his beer out of reach, 'you'll have to find somewhere else to drink.'

Briar's threat was hollow; Law couldn't afford to drink anywhere else but the Bucket. The Marinelle across town was for Lord Harrison and other dignitaries; folks like Lawrence Reed couldn't even set foot on the doorstep without an explicit invitation. Not that he'd go there anyway.

Law stretched a hand towards Briar, palm up and expectant. With the faintest of smiles cracking her hard face, the alchemist reached into the front of her blouse and lifted a necklace up and over her head. She placed the chain and key into Law's waiting hand.

'Take what you need from the cellar.'

THE WINE CELLAR, DESPITE being exactly what it claimed to be, housed more than The Dripping Bucket's surplus liquor stores and was the worst kept secret in Copperton. Every second day a note was pinned to the door, requesting a meeting with Briar for *personal business* despite the thinly maintained pretence that she was *just a tavern owner*. While alchemy and other such questionable practices were not outlawed, they weren't exactly sanctioned either. But, like everything else that went on in Copperton, so long as it did not bother Lord Harrison, he was willing to turn a blind eye.

Law coughed as he descended into the musty basement, displacing motes of dust as his boots touched the stairs. Barrels of whisky and ale were stacked high along the walls, and rows of bottle-heavy shelves disguised the room's depth. Everyone knew this was Briar's workshop, but to keep the tools of her trade hidden from sight, a false wall had been installed so it appeared to hold nothing more valuable than its oldest oak cask. But Law—and a handful of other favoured investigators, he supposed—knew which cabinets had been set on wheels and which barrels to roll aside to find her *other* wares.

At the back of the cellar, Briar had built herself a lab. A long table laden with gas burners, test tubes and other alchemical paraphernalia made the whole space feel cramped and chaotic. Notebooks filled with scribbles lay open and stained, and a thick dark liquid had been left distilling in a bulbous glass beaker over a low flame. Law's lips drew back in a grimace at the acrid stench and he brought a fresh kerchief to his nose. If this is what Briar needed liver for, he certainly hoped the client who'd come to her for aid wasn't supposed to consume it.

Law did his best to ignore the smell and set to locating the tools required to delicately harvest an organ. He never had much use for small blades in his line of work, relying solely on his pistol for protection. It hung heavy in its holster as he picked up an array of scalpels and slipped them into the leather satchel slung across his shoulder. He also took a jar prefilled with ethanol for transporting the liver back to Briar's stores.

There was no thrill in such a menial, distasteful errand, but he needed to remain in Briar's good graces. Investigators had a way of ending up in Copperton and there were now too many cooks in the kitchen. He wasn't one to kiss arse, but if it meant being first in line for whatever job arose next, he'd pucker up all the same. Work had been scarce of late, and there was only so far he could stretch his luck before creditors came knocking.

Law was half-tempted to swipe a bottle for company on the road but thought better of it. His gut roiled at the prospect of dissecting a fresh corpse and he didn't need to upset it further with too much liquor. Instead, he quietly locked the door behind him, slipped the key into his shirt and gave a perfunctory glance over each shoulder before stepping out into the street.

There was little traffic at this hour, too late for people to be wandering the streets but too early for revellers to be heading home. Law doffed his hat to the occasional passing carriage but otherwise moved unnoticed, guided by the light of the lantern hooked over his belt. It was an old brass bull's eye lantern Briar had liberated from the disused watchman's box after Lord Harrison rescinded funding for a night-time guard, citing lack of need. For a time, Briar had an investigator or two keep an eye on the more mundane happenings in Copperton but eventually she, too, abandoned the practice.

'Monsters are simple,' she always said. 'They have patterns. Rules. Instincts. Humans are chaos. Let someone else deal with them.'

Law still balked at that decision. How many murders went unsolved because the viscount didn't give a shit about what went on under his very nose? Briar brought justice to those tormented by the unnatural, but what recompense awaited victims of mortal crimes? Who punishes those who leave bodies to rot in the Taschenwilde?

Or those sent to harvest their organs?

Law pushed the thought aside and chose instead to be grateful for the lantern that would have otherwise gone to waste. The wide, steady beam of light left his hands free for dealing with any unexpected *problems* he might encounter on his journey to the edge of town.

The road through the Taschenwilde had been gated long before Law came to Copperton. Anyone travelling to Sunscourt was instead forced to circle hundreds of miles around the sprawling forest, adding days, if not weeks, to their journey. The town's upper class, who were conditioned to believe their coin would buy them anything, decried the superstitious coachmen who refused to take the once cobbled and lamp-lined highway, now in considerable disrepair. Occasionally, inflated remuneration enticed the young or the desperate to take the shortcut through the Taschenwilde; many did not return. Law and others like him had investigated the disappearances but never found evidence of foul play. They were simply gone. Many concluded they'd escaped to the capital, their ill-fated journey through the forest but a ruse to distance themselves from whatever miserable life they'd fled. Still, the disappearances were numerous enough to sway the wealthy into taking the long way around like everybody else.

It had never been enough to convince Briar, though. She knew the Taschenwilde was dangerous because it grew along a ley line—a vein beneath the world, rich with supernatural energy. It drew the unnatural towards it, like sawdust soaking up blood on the floor of The Dripping Bucket. Law wasn't sensitive to the pulse like Briar was, couldn't tap into its power like a conjurer or a soothsayer. But he knew it was there. Saw the power it offered—the damage it caused—and understood why people like him existed in places like this.

As he approached the edge of the forest, Law expected to find two sets of tracks heading into the Taschenwilde: one for whoever dumped the body, and another for whoever found it. Instead, there was only a single set. It could have been one and the same, he supposed; it wouldn't be first time a murderer tried to seem innocent by reporting the crime they committed. But apprehending a murderer was not what he was being paid to do, even if his instincts urged him to look for clues and motive. Besides, the prints were small enough they likely belonged to one of Briar's little rats. Whatever they'd discovered must have been cut and dry; he'd best keep to the task at hand and not get distracted by *what ifs*.

Brambles clawed at his long, heavy jacket, oiled to protect against the wet. Law held the lantern aloft now, illuminating the path forward as best he could. Vision was poor in the Taschenwilde, impeded by a fog that never lifted regardless of the weather beyond the forest. Mist curled at his ankles, obscuring the tracks in the undergrowth. He didn't see any blood—old or otherwise. Either the body was long dead before it was dumped here or...

Harvest the liver. That's the job. Procure, not ponder.

It wasn't a surprise when Law stumbled upon the corpse less than a hundred yards from the forest's edge. It was further than most dared to explore, deeper than most bothered to trek to simply dispose of a body. Law set his lantern down on a rock beside the corpse, attempting to illuminate the small clearing. It had been a child, he realised, mouth turning dry—a girl. Her cropped blonde hair was matted with mud and twigs; blood dried on her chin and chest, having spilled in torrents from her mouth. Whatever killed her sure had been violent.

Crouching, Law slipped the satchel off his shoulder and unloaded the specimen jar with care, setting out the scalpels on the rock to prepare for the extraction. His breath plumed as a sudden chill rolled in around him. The darkness of the Taschenwilde was so oppressive he could see nothing but a black smear below the child's head, shadows stretching eerily with the lantern's meagre glow. Law brought the light closer to the body, ready to make the first incision.

And stopped.

The girl's belly was exposed to the night, flesh peeled back like ribbons around an empty abdominal cavity. It gaped at him like an open mouth, frozen in a scream. Visceral panic took hold of Law and he lost his balance, falling back on his arse in shock. The white of her spine glistened within, blood, organ and tissue all but sucked dry. Law drew in a breath, holding the rising bile in his throat, as he slipped a hand into the exposed cavern.

Gone. It was all gone.

Liver, stomach, kidneys. Bowel. Uterus. Pancreas. Spleen.

Heart.

Law snatched back his hand and wiped it briskly on the front of his jacket. Rage and revulsion washed over him. Briar's reconnaissance runners had given her one hell of a half-arsed report! He should have brought knives, silver—something more than his pistol to protect against the supernatural.

He grabbed the lantern from its rock perch and washed the light over the girl's body—what was left of it, anyway—looking for bites. Werewolves were known for their love of human hearts, but he was certain he'd driven the last pack from town last year. They didn't usually strip the body dry like this, either. Something didn't add up. There were no bites—beast, insect or otherwise. He turned the girl's arm to inspect the inner stretch of her wrist, pausing as he caught a strange shadow on her palm. Bringing the lantern closer, Law flexed back her dead fingers for a better look.

It was a scar—an unnatural one at that. A nine-sided shape enclosed a tangle of intersecting lines that formed some sort of misshapen star—a pattern that had been *carved* into her flesh. Not too long ago either, judging by its deep, purple sheen. The same mark was on her other hand, as well.

Law scratched at his coarse stubble. He'd never seen anything like this before, never even heard of similar finds. The belly looked as if it had been peeled open like a fruit. Had something clawed its way out from the body? Or was this just the work of a sick man with a knife?

A shiver trembled across Law's skin. He lingered there a moment, crouched beside the body with a scalpel in one hand and lantern in the other. Eventually he swapped the blade and redundant specimen jar for a notebook and charcoal stick. Keeping the girl's palm in the light, he sketched the marking onto a new page, careful to capture its likeness accurately. Beside the diagram, he recorded notes of his finding: the missing organs, the girl's approximate age—twelve; fourteen at most—her location within the Taschenwilde...

He should bury the body, he knew, but hadn't brought the tools required for digging a grave. The soil beneath Law's feet was hard, compacted despite the ever-present moisture in the air. Scratching it aside with his fingernails wasn't like to achieve much. Besides, Briar might want to investigate the body herself. Walking back into town with a mutilated girl in his arms was bound to draw unwanted attention, though, and so, against his better instincts, it was best to leave her here.

For now.

Law was turning to leave when he saw it—a dark smear disturbing the leaf litter out of the corner of his eye. Shadows were tricky things, so far from the forest's edge. They moved and jittered like a knave's nerves, never settling in one place, sometimes falling in ways that made one see things that weren't there.

But Law knew blood when he saw it.

The trail led towards the body—no, *away* from it. Not the girl's blood, then. Had she maimed her attacker before she died? He directed the lantern light towards the forest floor but it was hard to see if there'd been a struggle, now that his own boot prints trampled the clearing. He moved closer to inspect the dried blood that spread across the dirt and fallen leaves like butter over toast. Something had been dragged away.

Law pulled his pistol from its holster and edged along the new trail. A high-pitched shriek tore the night. He whirled the lantern around the clearing, weapon cocked and ready. Couldn't see anything. He stepped deeper into the thicket and a wet squelch burst beneath his boot. Another shriek.

Law jumped back and saw a bloodied tangle of rope crushed into the mud by his weight. No—not a rope. A ...

An umbilical cord.

He retreated further, almost dropping the lantern. His eyes followed the coiled length of it through the misty undergrowth, bracing himself for whatever lay tethered to its end. There was a squeal, and something slithered out of sight; Law stomped his foot down on the cord, deliberately this time, preventing its escape.

Not a baby, then.

The creature thrashed and hissed, a slimy blur flailing in the leaf litter. It was the size of a newborn, but nothing human moved or sounded like that. And its appearance ...

Pallid grey flesh stretched across the body of a malformed amphibian caught between tadpole and frog. Three of its four eyes were swollen shut and the other bulged from the side of its head like a pit partway squeezed from an olive. High-pitched keening escaped its sphincter of a mouth as it writhed in the muck. The small, tight lips parted and closed—a fish gasping on the riverbank.

'What fucking hellhole did you crawl out of,' Law muttered, nose pinched in the crook of his elbow as he tried not to inhale its stink. Elor's balls, it was putrid. Slimy, rotten and malformed. He inched a little closer, looking for any defining features that could help identify it. But as he moved, the horizontal black slit of its one good eye suddenly widened. It sprang from the mud, lunged straight for Law. The tight seal of its lips found purchase on his neck. Law cursed viciously as he battered it aside with his pistol, the grip sinking into its gelatinous body. As it fell away, he caught a glimpse of row after row of tiny saw-blade teeth encircling its maw, which had widened like a flange as it latched onto his flesh.

Law pressed his fingers to his throat and found blood. Not much: the bite had been shallow, but it was swollen and bruised from the brief, intense suction. There was no time to inspect it further—the creature screeched and prepared to launch again.

Law raised his pistol. Pulled the trigger. The beast exploded in a shower of green and grey mucus and a last, agonised wail. Wiping ribbons of viscera from his eyes, Briar's investigator crouched among the slimy remains, looking for anything to salvage for her research. There wasn't much left. Whatever it was, it had been easy to kill, though he supposed it was just a juvenile.

'These the kind of monstrosities found along ley lines, then?' Law pondered aloud. 'Flesh-sucking demons? Or—'

He glanced back over his shoulder. At the young girl and her empty abdominal cavity—empty veins. Law touched his throat again, the phantom suction still tugging at his flesh.

'Fuck.'

Law went back to his satchel and pulled out the specimen jar. With care, he nestled it in the slop-soaked grass and unscrewed the lid. He hooked a length of the severed and limp umbilical cord over a stick and lowered it into the clear fluid. A thin film of tiny bubbles pimpled across the surface of the cord before dissipating as it settled into its suspended state.

Swinging the satchel over his shoulder, Law picked up the lantern and began the trudge back through the forest, pistol at the ready.

2

BUSINESS

DAWN WAS BREAKING BY the time Law made it back to his rooms. His house sat at the edge of the Chamberpots—a strip of rundown dwellings not considered a slum only because so many streets in Copperton looked just like it. The Chamberpots was named for its proximity to Lord Harrison's manor and was a convenient dumping ground for the viscount's waste buckets.

It took three heavy blows from Law's shoulder to barge through his front door. He stumbled inside as it finally gave way, dust and water-soft splinters bursting in a cloud. The coals in the hearth had gone cold, meaning the stew hanging in the pot would have congealed to a lumpy mess. Law couldn't bring himself to look at it, not with memories of that foetal monstrosity still wriggling around in his mind.

He shrugged out of his jacket, hung it on the peg behind the door, then unloaded his satchel and pistol onto the table. A cold shiver prickled across his skin as he removed the specimen jar from the battered old bag. The umbilical cord curled around itself like a hibernating serpent. Had it been coiled like that when he left the forest? He set it down in the centre of his table, using just the very tips of his fingers to settle it in place.

In any case, he was foul, covered head to toe in viscera and slop, and in dire need of a wash.

Law was not a vain man, but there was little he liked less than the filth of his work. He could abide stained clothes, unkempt hair, and a face several days past due for a shave, but monster muck on his skin was unforgivable.

The thought of his old tin tub filled with water was more inviting than it should have been considering the effort it would take to fill it from the water pump three houses down. He could sponge himself off in front of the hearth, as he usually did, but there was grime in his hair and beard and under his fingernails. He needed to bathe. Needed to wash it all off until its presence was just a memory. He could still feel the fibrous cord writhe under his boot and the sharp suction of the flanged mouth against his neck. Again, he touched the bruised, puckered skin where the creature had suckled at him. This time, his fingers came away dry; the small wound had scabbed.

Law pushed the memory out of his mind as he retrieved a bucket and commenced the tedious task of hauling water from the pump to fill his tub. It took several trips in the cold morning air, half-dressed as he was, but he was so desperate to rid himself of the night's filth he didn't much care. After giving his hands a quick scrub in the bitingly chill water, he stoked the hearth coals back to life, feeding the fire a log from his stash in the corner. Then, he swung the stew pot back over the flames to heat his dinner. Breakfast. Whatever.

The room was stuffy and reeked with the stench that had followed him home. Giving the jar a wide berth, Law leant over the table to open the shutters. False Elor, he smelt like death. Like stale blood and putrefaction and internal tissues unnaturally exposed to the air. In all his years as an investigator, he'd never seen a body like that before—not even victims of a back-alley hedgewitch with an enthusiastic penchant for the dark arts had their insides scraped clean like that.

Law undressed in a fury, tossing his clothes to the ground ,knowing full well the water in the tub would still be cold. He didn't care. The sooner he'd washed the night off his skin, the better. He stepped into the water with a hiss and quickly sat to toss his legs over the side. At least his feet would get warm, dangling by the hearth. He wasted no time scrubbing at his arms and nails with a wiry little brush until his skin turned red. Gingerly, he scraped the bristles over the wound on his neck, hissing at the sting. When it no longer hurt as much, he upended a pail of bathwater over his head and relaxed deeper into the tub, finally clean and content.

Until he realised his cigarillos were out of reach; Law snorted his frustration. Now the flash of intense repulsion had passed, he felt ... odd. Flat. Emotionally stretched. He'd been covered in monster muck many times, but never experienced the need to cleanse himself so vigorously. The foetus that had emerged from the Taschenwilde—from the *child*—unsettled him deeply, more than he thought anything still could. Yet again, he raised his fingers to the wound on his neck, hot and inflamed now it had been rubbed raw. If it were venomous, its toxins were slow acting. Aside from severe discomfort and fatigue, he was otherwise unaffected by the bite. A new breed of vampyr, then? A cold shiver raced across his flesh that had nothing to do with the water temperature. For someone who made a living hunting the ancient and arcane, *new* was never anything good.

A black cat with a single burst of white fur on its chest jumped in through the open window, emitting a curious yowl as it settled on the ledge. It was a stray who'd roamed the Chamberpots before coming to rely on Law for its meals. He supposed that meant the cat was his now, although he hadn't gotten around to giving it a name and probably never would. Black Cat seemed to serve just fine.

The cat let out a trill little chirp as it eyed the stew pot.

'Wait your turn,' Law insisted gruffly. 'I haven't eaten mine yet.'

Black Cat's tail lashed in response and Law took it as a sign it was time to get out. He was stiff from sitting in the cold water and rose with a groan that should have embarrassed someone of his years. At thirty-seven he was not exactly an *old* man, but his line of work had worn his body down faster than even the most punishing factory labour.

Shaking himself off by the fire like a dog, Law tossed his soiled shirt and trousers in the tub to soak. His oiled coat would need to be wiped clean but that could wait, despite the stink—food and fresh clothes first.

He owned little more than a handful of linen shirts and a couple of hard-wearing workman's pants. They were all so stained and worn that they never looked freshly laundered even when they were as clean as could be. There'd be a pair of trousers hanging up in his wardrobe; a shirt and coat too. But his stomach howled so viciously, dressing could wait.

Law padded towards the hearth, grateful for the warmth on his goose-pimpled skin. Water dripped from the ends of his dark hair, hanging in thick curls past his shoulders, as he leant forward to stir the stew, keeping his groin as far back from the coals as possible. The food boiled heartily and the melted fat gave it an appealing shine, unlike the dull, hard mess it had been when he arrived home. He brought the spoon to his lips for a taste, hissing as a dollop splashed on his naked chest.

From the windowsill, Black Cat spat and bellowed a defensive rumble from deep in its gullet. Law turned, expecting to find the cat protesting the stolen mouthful of food. Instead, the creature was wide eyed, its fur ruffled and back arched, looking for a fight.

All this for days' old stew?

But the cat wasn't looking at Law's meal. Its gold-green gaze was fixed on the specimen jar, at the shrivelled umbilical cord that was—that was *moving*.

Law tumbled away from the hearth, lunging for his pistol. By the time he rolled back to his feet, the hammer was cocked and ready to ignite. The lead pellet shattered the glass jar and shot through the cabin's thin wall. Black Cat screeched and sprang from the window ledge, streaking off down the street.

Law wiped the trickling water from his forehead with the back of his arm and lowered the pistol. Glass shards littered the table like a bag of spilt grain; the ethanol dripped onto the floor; and the umbilical cord thrashed like an eel on a fisherman's chopping block, writhing its way across the tabletop.

Toward the open window.

With a great sweep of his arm, Law flung the cord back in a shower of broken glass. It landed on the hearth stones and its wet, fleshy body sizzled against the heat. A high-pitched keening filled the room; Law kicked it into the coals and watched as its death throes stilled, not satisfied until it was reduced to ash.

He exhaled heavily as the fight drained from his muscles. Instinctively, he gripped his forearm and looked down to see blood leaking between his fingers. He sucked a sharp breath in between his teeth and inspected the torn flesh for embedded shards. It was clean.

'Small mercies,' Law grumbled as he tip-toed around the broken glass on the floor to retrieve a bottle of whisky from the shelf. He pulled out the cork stopper with his teeth, spat it onto the table, and then took a long drink before sloshing it over the cuts. It chafed to see good booze used in such a manner, and it stung like a bastard, but he'd seen too many men lose limbs from innocuous wounds turned sour to risk leaving it uncleaned. Infection would cost more than his arm—it'd cost him his livelihood, too. Maybe even his life.

When the bottle was empty, Law retrieved the notebook from his satchel. He brushed aside the spilled ethanol and remaining glass to take a seat at the table and flick through the pages to where he'd recorded the night's findings. With his charcoal stick, he added more details to page—crude etchings of the body and the creature were the best he could manage from his memory. Only the peculiar scar found on the palms of her hands was rendered with any clarity. A nine-pointed star within a nine-sided polygon. The uneven number of spokes from each vertex left the shape out of balance and unlikely the work of an artist. A symbol for something, then?

But what does it represent?

With care, he tore the page from his notebook and set it aside. On a fresh sheet of paper, Law recreated the diagram several times over, adding additional lines and musings around each sketch. Was it incomplete? Not in any way Law could determine.

Irritation at the unknown soon got the better of him and he pushed the notebook and charcoal aside. Briar would know. Probably. He'd show her tomorrow. He folded the original drawing with his mission report for the old alchemist away in the satchel and reached for his bottle, forgetting it was empty. When his lips came away dry, he staggered light-headed and exhausted into the adjoining room.

The narrow space was dark—more a sleeping nook than a bedroom—with no windows to welcome the rising sun. His shins collided with the bed frame and he tumbled forward onto the hard mattress.

There was nothing left to do now but sleep.

A ROUGH WETNESS BRUSHING against his forehead stirred Law back to consciousness with alarm. He reached for his pistol and found nothing but the scratchy linen of his bedsheets. Panic burned brighter. By the time he was upright and scanning the room for danger, his pulse was thundering in his ears. A curious feline chirrup broke the tension.

'I've got nothing for you,' Law told Black Cat in defeat, opening his arms wide to emphasise the bareness of his home—and body. He squatted and the cat drew closer, brushing its cheek against Law's hand for a neck scratch.

'You really want some of that stew, huh?' he continued, fingers massaging the underside of the cat's jaw. Its purr reverberated up his arm, surprisingly loud. 'Too bad there's just enough left for me. But don't worry—I have to go report to Briar. Probably won't earn me much, but it might be enough to rummage up something for your dinner. Greedy little bugger.'

He dressed without hurry and returned to the chaos of the main room to retrieve his satchel. It was a rare bright day outside—fortunate, as he'd not yet wiped the filth from his overcoat. He made do with his old woollen waistcoat, unbuttoned, over his linen shirt.

With his clothes still soaking in the tub, Law would have to forego a shave. He palmed his face, finding the stubble thick but not wild. It'd suffice—it'd have to. Briar wouldn't care, and too bad if she did. It was not like anyone beyond the upper gentry cared about the supple cleanliness of a man's face. He quickly restrained his hair with a length of leather cord and slipped into his boots. They reeked of mud and peat from the Taschenwilde but there was little to be done about that now.

It was midafternoon, and although the day had looked cheery from the window, a fierce icy breeze cut him like the bullet tearing that foetal creature to shreds. Despite his hunger, he'd not had the stomach to eat, and the scent of sizzling meat and sticky pastries blowing down from the town square was a torment he didn't need. The streets buzzed: horse-drawn carriages clapped over the cobblestones and urchins flitted about, trying to swindle a coin or two from ignorant passersby. Traffic increased as he made his way from the Chamberpots into Copperton proper. It was market day and wooden carts with colourful awnings lined the street, peddling trinkets and exotic produce brought in from Sunscourt and beyond. Ladies in long skirts and white blouses milled about, all but blocking the road to Lord Harrison's manor. A scuffle was on the verge of erupting between an impatient coachman and a particularly obtuse chaperon accompanying his lady. Law turned into an alley to avoid the drama.

With the cheerful din of the bell, Law entered The Dripping Bucket and found it empty, save for a man passed out at the bar. Reynold, the day manager, was at the back of the room, disapproving scowl on his face as Satin, the resident bard, gestured emphatically to explain herself, breasts all but bouncing out of her loosely laced blouse. Defeated, Reynold shook his head and turned to greet Law.

'Wine cellar,' the rough old man said, thrusting a thumb back over his shoulder. He muttered something to himself about there never being any real customers during the day.

'Mr Carter, I'm terribly sorry, but this is the chance of a lifetime. If you'd just let me explain—'

Law retreated before hearing anymore of the bard's plea and made his way down into the cellar. He was greeted by the pungent stench of burning hair and charred bone. Briar stood over an iron pot filled with flames, smoke rising in dark plumes to choke the enclosed space.

'You really should put in that second chimney,' he said by way of greeting.

The acerbic old woman coughed and waved smoke from her face. 'Elor's fucking balls, boy, don't sneak up on me like that!'

'I was hardly sneaking. Your hearing finally giving out?'

'Oh, fuck you, I'm a spring chicken compared to that crone Maisley in Ellersparke.' She waved another cloud of smoke away, attempting to usher it out the narrow open window above her table. 'Hmm, got more than I need,' she muttered, stoking the pot fire by feeding a stiffened rat to the flames. 'That old ginger tom is a bloody good mouser. Want some for your little thing?' She gestured at two dead rodents on the table beside her.

'I don't have a cat,' Law insisted, but swept the dead vermin into his satchel anyway. 'What are you doing?'

'Making corpse dust,' Briar replied with a nonchalant shrug. 'Been a request for it. Some superstitious dullard up on Merigold Lane paid me a whole gold coin to make something they could easily do themselves.'

'Thought corpse dust was made from human remains.'

'It is, if you need to ward against the evil and vengeful—not whatever run-of-the-mill poltergeist Lady Avery has flitting about her estate.'

Law smelt a job. 'Has someone been to investigate her holdings?'

Briar spun on her heels, eyes narrowing. 'You're here fishing for more jobs and yet you stand before me empty-handed. Where's my liver? And the specimen jar and scalpels you took? You can't keep losing my tools, Mr Reed, and expecting not to pay for it.'

'Jar's broken,' Law explained flatly, reaching into his satchel. 'And there was no liver to be harvested.' He passed the notebook page to Briar. As she unfolded it, he continued, 'The body cavity was empty. All of it—gone. What kind of hack apprentice do you have running reconnaissance? There was nothing normal about that corpse and they should have told you so.'

Briar's jaw hardened as she observed the proffered sheet of paper. 'Elor's teeth...' she whispered.

'My first thought was werewolves,' Law said. 'Then a rather en-thusiastic hedgewitch dumping their scraps. But there were these marks—' he pointed out the diagram of the nine-pointed star '—on her hands, that I'd never seen before.'

Briar suddenly dropped the sketch into the pot fire. The edges of the paper glowed red before igniting and crumpling into powdery flakes of ash.

'No,' Briar said with finality. 'No. This is not a job for us.'

'What the fuck, Briar—the hell it's not. Something came out of that little girl. Some kind of monster. It ate her and then it tried to eat me.' He gestured to the puckered wound on his neck. Briar pushed his chin back to inspect it.

'You've suffered worse,' she said, dismissive.

Law slapped her hand away. 'I've never seen anything like it before. The way it fed. The way it moved. This is something new—something different.'

'Which is exactly why it's not our business,' the alchemist insisted. She clasped Law's hands within her own. 'Mr Reed, I've been at this job long enough to know what needs our attention and what doesn't. This was likely just a runaway girl whose unwanted pregnancy was mutated by the ley lines under the Taschenwilde. An unfortunate and unnatural phenomenon, yes, but not one that needs to be investigat-ed.'

She stepped back to blow on the now smouldering embers,cooling them to little more than smoke and ash.

But Law was not prepared to let it go. 'Those scars weren't natural, Briar. Someone put them there. Just like someone left that girl there to die. And I'm not even sure she was old enough to *be* pregnant. That's not what happened here, I can—'

'Regardless.' Briar raised a hand to silence him. 'People do all sorts of things to distract themselves from pain, Mr Reed. Even carve meaningless patterns into their flesh.'

It was a non-answer and they both knew it. He opened his mouth to protest once more but the look in Briar's eye told him it would cost more than his career as an investigator in Copperton.

'Get those rodents back to your cat, Mr Reed, before they start to stink up your bag,' she said coolly, head held high in victory. 'And come by the bar tomorrow. You can deliver this corpse dust to Lady Avery for me since you're so desperate for work that you're seeing jobs where there are none.'

Clenching his teeth on a reply, Law bobbed his head in farewell. Suspicion swarmed like a flies over a corpse as he left the wine cellar, his frustration too raw to even glance back over his shoulder. He would not let his go, and he couldn't fathom how Briar was prepared to. There was a cover-up here—a mystery he'd have to solve. And he would.

Even if he had to do it alone.

3

POLTERGEIST

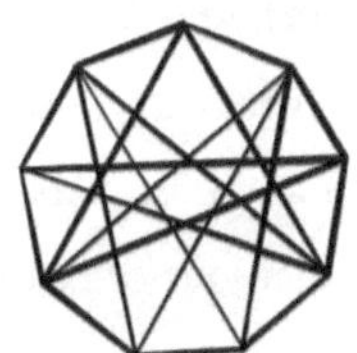

LAW DRAGGED HIMSELF BACK to The Dripping Bucket right on noon the next day, his petty irritation at Briar preventing him from getting there at first light. The front door was still locked, an ambiguous "Come Back Later" scrawled on a wooden sign hanging from the knocker.

Law took himself round back to the service door that was always irresponsibly left open. Inside, Reynold spread a fresh layer of sawdust across the floor with a mangled iron rake. He looked at Law in exasperation.

'You can't just let yourself in as you please, Mr Reed,' he moaned. 'We got rules, you know.'

'Ms Loren asked me to meet her here,' Law said as he slipped onto his usual stool. He took out his cigarillos.

With a resigned sigh, Reynold leant the rake against the wall, took his apron from a peg by the door and stepped behind the bar. He poured Law a well-watered beer and slid it across the polished wood.

'On yer tab then, Mr Reed?'

'Sure.' Law waited for a protest; it was likely still full. When Reynold said nothing, Law's chest relaxed and took a sip as he watched a young man with sandy hair tune a lyre at the far end of the Bucket. Elor's balls, he hadn't seen a lyre in years; wandering minstrels and their humble strings had fallen out of favour with the noble courts, who these days preferred to read the gossip on the printed pages of a daily circular than listen to a song. Many taverns still employed a musician, though, even the Bucket, hence this sad little fellow with his stained vest and busted lyre. Lutes were more common now, but even they were a paltry imitation of what the finer establishments offered.

'What happened to the woman?' Law asked, pointing his chin at the boy as he propped his elbows on the bar behind him.

'The Marinelle just got a harpiscorde,' Reynold said ina bitter rumble. 'That slimy bard, Hollyhock or whatever his damn name is, offered our Satin a duet three nights a week. Her big break, she reckons.'

The boy yelped as a snapped string kissed his fingertip.

'False Elor help us.' The old man shook his head and resumed his preparations for the mid-afternoon opening. 'Should've let her stay on the rest of the week like she offered. Damn pride got the best of me.'

'Briar wouldn't want a part-time minstrel,' Law scoffed. 'Nor would she pay more for one who didn't want to stay. We'll get used to this one, I'm sure.'

'Don't think the lads will be too interested in ogling this one, Mr Reed. Not the way they did Satin.'

Law hummed deep in his throat and drained the last of his weak beer. He finished a second before Briar arrived for their meeting, her mousy hair loosely tied without braids giving her a soft appearance Law hadn't expected. She placed a parcel of brown paper on the bar beside the empty glasses.

'I'm really running another errand?' he huffed, eyeing the package. When Briar had asked him to deliver an order of corpse dust to Lady Avery, he thought it'd been a jest. Maybe it was a punishment instead.

Briar looked left and right. 'I don't see any other investigators here this afternoon.'

Soft, but still thorny.

Law exhaled a plume of cigarillo smoke. Dare he ask for compensation?

The alchemist's eyes narrowed as she caught his probing stare. "I'll make good on the promise to wipe your tab. And give you the dregs of the soup pot to take home.'

'A bronze.'

'To walk a packet of dust up the hill?' Briar snorted. 'May as well do it myself.'

'Two coppers,' Law conceded. 'And the soup.'

The alchemist's lips sharpened to a thin line. Her hand slipped into the pocket of her apron and produced a mangled copper coin, the edges well shaved back.

'The rest when you get back,' she said, a note of challenge in her voice. Having had nothing to show for his last job—and breaking one of her specimen jars—Law wasn't surprised to see the bristly old broad adopt such a hard-nosed approach. There was a bitter sting to it, though; Law was a persistent and reliable investigator, but he'd botched things before, just like any other man. She was sending him a message, one he heard loud and clear: *don't question my judgement.*

That didn't stop the incident going around and around his head like a millstone. The horror of the unknown, the rising suspicion over Briar's dismissive behaviour ... he couldn't leave it alone. But he had to make Briar believe he had.

Law pocketed the coin and held the alchemist's gaze with a forced but affable smile. 'And where will I find the lovely Lady Avery?'

MERIGOLD CRESCENT WAS A cul-de-sac of wealthy homesteads off a cobbled road that wound up the hill towards the northern edge of Viscount Harrison's estate. Each property held small acreage—for hunting and riding, not farming—and the pseudo town square their houses convened around provided little reason for the neighbourhood gentry to mingle with the working class below.

Law's visits to Merigold Crescent were few and far between; rather than hire an investigator to see to the unusual or unexplained, they preferred to spend their money on trinkets and potions to ward off *evil.*

'This amulet is from Coronundronn, the continent to the north,' he'd heard one lady claim of her necklace the last time he'd run deliveries for Briar. 'It protects against illness. I've not been sick a day since I got it.'

The locket was a simple pomander filled with herbs, likely assembled by a local hedgewitch. She'd have paid through the nose for such a charm; to have something unique and mysterious was a valuable asset to these people. If only they knew the very real dangers that people like him dealt with. The tools of his trade were not to display like trophies in a cabinet.

The Avery residence was a three-level terracotta manor covered in vines. Smoke billowed from chimneys either end of the high-pitched roof, and its small door was almost lost in the deeply shadowed entrance wrought in polished white stone. A curved turret with a sharp spire swelled off the front west corner, facing the road.

Wealthier than I thought.

The ornate iron gate was ajar; Law shouldered it open to step onto a pebbled path that crunched with dry leaves. The groundskeepers had been lax and the first signs of neglect crept into the flower beds with weeds popping their ugly heads up between the blooms.

There was a strange aura about the place—a gloom that hung heavy and low like an invisible fog. It set Law's nerves on edge, just like the Taschenwilde after dark.

Something wasn't right here.

Law shifted the parcel of corpse dust to one hand and rapped his knuckles on the door, realising too late there was a large brass knocker right in the centre. He was about to raise it for a follow-up tap when he caught the whisper of footsteps inside. The door swung open to a tall woman in a sharply tailored black dress and crisp white apron. She was severe but well presented—not dissimilar to Briar in that regard—and held herself with all the certainty of a woman in charge. Her silent stare demanded explanation as to his presence.

'Package for Lady Avery,' Law said.

The housemistress gave a curt nod and reached for the parcel; Law shrugged aside.

'For her hands only,' he insisted.

'Lady's indisposed.'

'This'll help with that.'

Her lips cut an even thinner line across her face as she struggled to suppress her irritation. Law braced for a slamming door. Fool—what did it matter if the parcel came to Lady Avery by way of her maid?

The door started to close. He was about to plead his case further when a voice called from the top of the stairs, 'Let him in, Meredith.'

'Of course, ma'am.' The housemistress retreated and gestured for Law to enter, bowing her head as he passed. Law doffed his hat and scraped his boots on the mat before stepping over the threshold.

Lady Avery was a petite woman with pale blue eyes and softly curled golden hair that was loosely restrained at the nape of her neck. She was not old—of an age with Law, perhaps—but torment marked her face with deep lines and dark circles. Despite bidding him welcome, Lady Avery was not dressed to receive guests: the rose-coloured robe draped atop her white nightgown suggested a woman who had, until very recently, been abed.

'Meredith, bring tea to the sitting room,' Lady Avery said as she descended into the foyer, delicate hand trailing the banister for support.

'I'm not here to intrude,' Law began, proffering the parcel before Lady Avery interjected.

'And you're not. I insist. Meredith, the tea.'

She passed like a winter wind into the room on the right, leaving Meredith to hurry off in a tizz. Equally off guard, Law followed Lady Avery and found her seated in a high-backed upholstered armchair by the fire, slippered feet propped up on a low stool.

'Take a seat, Mr...?' She trailed off but gestured at the empty chair all the same.

'Reed. Lawrence Reed. I have a delivery from Briar Loren,' he said, stretching past Lady Avery to place the package on the table beside her. 'I trust you know its contents.' He retreated to his own chair and took a seat, resting his hat atop his knee.

Avery folded her hands in her lap. 'Oh, yes. That,' she mumbled, distant. Her eyes shifted towards the mantlepiece, where several dark portraits lined up in frames. 'That might help.'

'Do you want to tell me what's going on?'

Meredith entered with a tray, the crockery clinking as she set it down to pour two cups of steaming tea. Their conversation came to a halt. Once alone, Lady Avery asked, 'Do you read the papers, Mr Reed?'

'I don't make it a habit, no.'

Silence filled the space between them. Avery stirred in two lumps of sugar and clinked the spoon on the side of the delicate china. She took a long sip, watching Law over the rim with an unwavering, measured stare. Law left his untouched; he had no taste for botanical brews.

'Camelia Avery,' she said. 'My daughter. Missing almost four months. Would have been thirteen last week.' Her pale gaze once again flicked to a portrait on the mantel—a blonde girl set in a gilded frame. The resemblance struck Law immediately. He hadn't seen it when he first looked at Lady Avery, but now that he saw her features in a daughter, he couldn't help but recall the body from the Taschen-wilde. It was hard to be sure—he'd not spent long observing the girl's *face*—but there were enough similarities for the suspicion to take root in his mind. The age matched, and the girl in the forest had almost certainly been blonde. Was her nose rounded like a little button? Had her jawline been as sharp?

Law moistened his lips and shifted in his chair as Lady Avery's lower lip quivered like a butterfly wing before she turned her face away. Law found this the hardest part of his job: the unbridled emotion of clients riddled with grief. It wasn't something he came across every day, not in places like Copperton. No one wore smiles or let tears glisten on their cheeks. They got you nothing in the poorer parts of town. Nothing but a target on your back for more pain. Better to curl the lip, deepen the scowl, and keep everyone else away.

Law poured himself some tea to alleviate the discomfort haemor-rhaging from the silence. Lady Avery blotted the inner corners of her eyes with her napkin, sniffed back the dripping mucus, and regained her composure.

'Camelia was...' Lady Avery continued, voice thick and hoarse. 'Well, she'd been out in the fields with her dog when I last saw her. Picking wildflowers or finding mushrooms or something—anything that would have got her hands dirty. She'd always come home in such a state.' Avery made a strange little sound somewhere between a sob and a chuckle.

'You think someone took her?' Law prompted.

She shook her hair. 'At first, I thought she'd just lost track of time. Camelia was always an absent sort of child—never really there, if you know what I mean. Not simple but ... different. She didn't get on well with the other girls in the lane. Wasn't fond of needlepoint or pianoforte. It was all books or wandering with that one.'

Law raised a finger, excusing himself for a moment, as he rummaged inside the breast pocket of his jacket for his notebook and charcoal stick. 'May I?' he asked, dipping his head towards the portrait on the mantel.

The lady's eyes narrowed. 'Whatever for?'

'To capture her likeness,' Law said, charcoal stick poised and ready. 'To help me look for her.'

'It's been four months, Mr Reed,' she scoffed, almost affronted at his suggestion. 'Four months is an awfully long time for a young girl to be missing. I know she's dead. Even if Winston won't believe it, I *know* she is. Why else would I want corpse dust?'

Law took down some quick notes and sketched a vague portrait of the girl on the mantel. The fact Avery was being haunted only made him more certain Camelia was the girl in the Taschenwilde. Poltergeists were born of violent death—it certainly fit the profile.

'Corpse dust won't bring you closure, Lady Avery,' Law said. 'But I can. If Miss Camelia is truly dead, then I will put her at peace so *you* can be at peace.'

Lady Avery shook her head, a despondent look in her eyes. 'I will never be at peace,' she said, voice cold and hard. 'Not without knowing what happened to her.'

'Then I'll find those answers, too.'

'Don't play with me, Mr Reed. I am too tired to be seduced by hope. I know what it is you and Briar Loren do. I implored her to help me once before, when Camelia first went missing. She turned me away and still demanded I pay for the little help she was. I refused and she—well, I'm rather surprised she sold me corpse dust.'

Law pondered the new information silently as he put the finishing touches on the sketch of the missing girl. Could this truly be a coincidence, and Camelia was just an unfortunate victim of *human* evil? She certainly wouldn't be the first grieving client Briar had turned away, refusing to solve the crimes the Crown Order were paid to look into. But if the girl in the Taschenwilde truly was Camelia, was Briar specifically ignoring *this* case? And why?

Law set down the charcoal, folded the notebook closed and looked across at Lady Avery. 'Let me look around the house. The fields as well—especially where Miss Camelia was last seen. I know a great deal of time has passed, but there may yet be clues that were overlooked.'

Lady Avery nodded with only slight hesitation.

'Yes, yes of course,' she said. 'I've not touched a thing in Camelia's room since she vanished. Winston insists I not even go in there. Doesn't want it disturbed. Perhaps he thinks she's still coming home, poor fool.' She made that scoffing sound again. 'So, please. Start wherever you like.'

She lowered her feet from the footstool and made to stand, as if she expected he commence investigating this very minute.

Law stuffed the notebook back inside his jacket and stood just as she did. 'Lady Avery. These investigations are best done alone. If you wish my help, then these terms are non-negotiable. I do not work with a chaperone.'

She pursed her lips; Law braced for the inevitable protest.

'You'll have to come back after dark, once Winston is asleep. He cannot know you are here. I trust you'll be very quiet.'

'As quiet as a ghost, ma'am,' Law said, bowing his head.

After accepting a purse of silver coins—with much more to follow, she assured him—Law slunk away to the field behind the Avery estate. This was an area best explored while he still had the light of day, meagre as it was through the thin cloud cover that had blown across from the west.

The paddock was overgrown, its low stone fences hidden beneath grass and foliage that reached well up Law's thighs. No livestock had grazed here for some time, if in fact they ever had. What exactly did the Averys have all this land for?

The far edge of the field backed onto a thickly wooded grove, too far from the Taschenwilde and ley line to be considered a supernatural point of interest. Still, if Law had learned anything about forests, it was that they were good for hiding bodies—and were not the kind of places people often ventured into alone.

With almost four months having passed since Camelia's disappearance, there were no longer any tracks to follow. Any grass trampled by her wandering feet had long since regrown; judging by the vastly undisturbed foliage, she was only one of a few who made use of the Averys' paddock. There was the odd rabbit warren, a fox trail or two, but nothing to indicate any sort of predator large enough to subdue a child.

Law paused before the thicket of ash and oak. Strange that this little patch endured, when much of the surrounding area had been cleared for the landed gentry. Despite its distance from the Taschenwilde, something about this copse made his hair stand on end. Memories of the body in the wood filtered back into his mind. This felt more than a coincidence. The corpse had a distinct likeness to Camelia. Age, too. The body was not long dead either, which would explain why Lady Avery would need corpse dust so long after her disappearance. The haunting must have only just begun. Was the spirit haunting the house ... or the parents?

Could Briar's theory about the creature be correct? Had the Averys cast her out when the truth of her condition could no longer be hidden, and claimed her a runaway? Is that why Winston Avery discouraged his wife's investigations? No—four months was not long enough to bring a pregnancy to term.

If she'd ever been pregnant at all...

Law clenched his fists. Opened them. Took a deep, slow breath. Exhaled.

This was not the time to be swept up in theories. The evidence would speak for itself—he just had to find it.

He continued into the thicket and found it more densely wooded than he'd first thought. Dead, fallen trees were home to fungi and moss, and the rotten wood sent a wet, earthy scent up his nostrils. It was not as viscerally unsettling as the Taschenwilde, but there was enough unease to send goosepimples across his flesh.

The afternoon sun filtered through the canopy in bright columns, momentarily blinding Law as he passed through them and back into the shadows.

His boot hit something squishy.

Bile rose up his throat as he reached for his pistol, bracing himself for a shrill shriek of agony. Hand on weapon, he glanced down at his feet, looking for an umbilical cord and instead found a greyish smear under the toe of his boot.

A mushroom. Or a toadstool—he never could tell. Law scraped his foot back through the undergrowth to wipe the muck off his sole. He'd narrowly missed stepping on another ... and another. Side by side they grew, pale little sentinels stretching around in a ring. At the opposite side of the circle, a gnarled old tree twisted out of the mossy ground, its blood-red berries bright against the darkness of the grove.

Panic rose in his chest as he finally pinpointed the reason for his discomfort. His dark eyes absorbed the broken ring of mushrooms and their place beneath the hawthorn bush. He swallowed and took a step back.

'Fuck.'

4
FALSE GOD

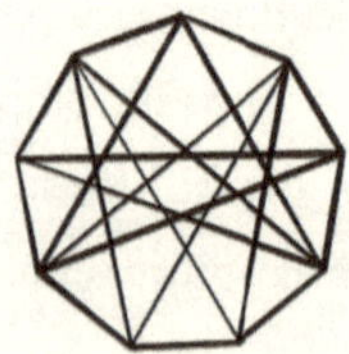

Briar didn't turn at the accusatory note in Law's voice. Just stood there stirring the large cast iron pot on the stove, watching the gravy thicken as she added a thin stream of flour.

'More than warrants an investigation,' Law continued with little tact. 'Did you even ask why Lady Avery wanted corpse dust?'

'Mr Reed, if I asked that of every client who came to my doorstep, I'd be sent to the gallows for accessory to murder,' Briar said thornily.

'Avery gets haunted the same time a young girl's body is found in the Taschenwilde. How can you not think it's related?'

'Coincidences happen.'

'The fuck they do. Not when the fae are involved.'

"

Briar released a short, sharp laugh. 'There's been no *aes sidhe* protecting that tree for years.'

Law paused at the use of such an archaic term. It was accurate, however; the last reported sightings of the faerie folk in Copperton were as old as the name itself.

'There was a faerie ring,' he said. 'A fresh one—alive. I, uh, stepped on it.'

The alchemist snorted. 'Stay away from the card table, then.'

She tapped the large wooden spoon twice on the side of the pot then set it down on a small dish. She swiped her finger through the soup cooling on the spoon and brought it to her mouth to taste.

'Hmm,' she said. 'Needs salt.'

Law stepped aside as she pushed past him. The bag of salt had been left open on the bench, beneath bunches of herbs strung out to dry. Aromas of thyme, rosemary and sage wafted through the room. Briar sprinkled a pinch over the thick surface of the stew and then wiped her hands on her apron. Far too blase about his revelations for Law's liking.

'Why are you avoiding this case?' he asked. 'You dismissed Camelia's disappearance and now a young girl is dead. Did you know about the hawthorn tree? Did you even look?'

'*Mr Reed.*' Briar spun to face him, the fire of irritation ablaze her in eyes. 'I have been investigating since you were little more than a dream in your mother's womb. I gave the Avery disappearance as much attention as I would any other mystery that finds its way to my doorstep. And there was nothing paranormal about it. You think only faeries and changelings steal little girls, Mr Reed? I did not teach you to be so naive. Camelia Avery's disappearance was a tragic one, but one wrought by mortal men. Just like your girl in the Taschenwilde—if they aren't one and the same!'

Law gritted his teeth, biting back words that would serve no purpose now. Was Briar that determined to throw him off the scent of the strange foetal monster he'd uncovered in the forest? Could she not admit she'd failed? That he'd found something she'd overlooked?

Taking a deep breath, Law dropped his gaze from Briar's challenging glare. He would not win this.

'Lady Avery has already paid,' he said wearily. 'I'm going to look into this for her.'

'It's up to you how you waste your time, Mr Reed, not me,' Briar retorted stiffly. 'But consider yourself off my books.'

'Ms Loren—'

'You've found this job on your own. I'm sure you'll find another.'

'Briar, please—'

'You can see yourself out now.'

Briar turned her attentions back to seasoning the stew, the room suddenly so silent he could hear the thick, boiling bubbles bursting in the pot. Law exhaled out of his nose, jaw clenched tight like his fists. Nothing he could say now would change Briar's mind.

With a dip of his head, he backed wordlessly out of the kitchen and back into the tavern, which was starting to fill with the evening's patrons. Briar would be busy at the Bucket until well into the night, leaving the wine cellar and its resources unattended. Law paused in the doorway, glancing back over his shoulder as he considered the consequences of stealing from the alchemist of Copperton. He really would be unemployed if he were caught—run out of town, even. But he was so sure there was something here Briar had overlooked; he couldn't let it go without proof.

Assuming a well-practiced casual gait, Law left The Dripping Bucket and headed round back to the external entrance to Briar's hidden alchemy lab. It faced away from Copperton's main thoroughfare, towards an overgrown vegetable garden and small animal pen belonging to a disused dwelling at the edge of the Taschenwilde. Despite the unlikelihood of anyone seeing him, apprehension jittered up Law's spine like a hoard of ants spilling from their nest. He took his picks from a leather pouch on his belt and fiddled with the lock. It clicked open with surprising ease and Law slipped inside, expelling his long-held breath with a rush.

Despite the chaos of her lab, Briar was a meticulous woman who kept a detailed catalogue of past and present clients—including investigations she'd conducted herself before retiring into a quasi-broker for the paranormal. Her immaculately organised archives lined the wall left of her alchemy room and spanned a good twenty years of history. But her unsolved cases she kept hidden on a shelf beneath the workbench, in sturdy cardboard boxes topped up with junk.

Law crouched and brushed aside the cobwebs to find a box labelled AVERY, filled with everything Briar had collected during her investigation: leather folders bound with cord; notebooks filled with clippings and sketches; and a sprig of hawthorn, the berries all dry and woody.

'Guess she found the tree,' Law muttered to himself as he pulled the box out onto the floor. He picked up the topmost journal, started leafing through the pages. It contained articles from the Copperton papers dated around the time of Camelia's disappearance, along with an etching of a very sullen Lord and Lady Avery. He scrutinised the picture. Noted the way Lady Avery covered most of her face with a handkerchief, and the whiff of a bad smell that tugged at her husband's nose.

'Hardly the figure of grief.' Law tucked the journal inside his jacket and bundled what else he could reasonably carry; Briar would notice a whole box removed from her archives, but she wouldn't miss an old book or two. At least, he hoped she wouldn't.

Law locked the wine cellar behind him and made his way across town, slowing to a stop once turning onto the Chamberpots. A hatted man with a double-breasted jacket and cane stood on his front step, thumping his knuckles against the rotting wood of the door.

'Good day, Mr Tillmann,' Law said with as much grace he could muster for his landlord.

The old man turned at Law's approach, his gnarled knuckles tightening on the ball of his walking stick. Pale eyes peeking out from his heavy brow like luminescent mushrooms beneath a fallen tree. He was a horrible man—one of Viscount Harrison's cronies—and if Law had the luxury of renting elsewhere, he most certainly would.

'It's most decisively *not* a *good day*, Mr Reed,' Tillmann said pointedly, the lines of his face deepening with his scowl. 'You are overdue on your rent, and I have had to come here to retrieve it.'

Today of all days, Law groaned to himself, acutely aware of the weighty coin purse jangling in his pocket. If Tillmann hadn't come here *today*, he wouldn't have had to lie. Could have made the same penniless excuse he always did. But for all his flaws, Law was honest. And that meant he had to pay his rent.

'I was just on my way to pay you,' Law said, rearranging the folders in his hands to retrieve his keys. Tillmann stepped aside to allow Law access to the door but otherwise seemed in no hurry to leave.

Law barged the door open and set the files down on the table. Tillmann peered in the open door, sneer on his lips as his rheumy eyes washed over the disarray. Law'd not yet emptied the wash tub, his clothes from his venture to the Taschenwilde still soaking in the now grey water. Broken glass pebbled the tabletop, though he'd done his best to sweep up any underfoot.

'It may not be the most luxurious of dwellings, Mr Reed, but I expect it to be well kept,' Tillmann huffed, indignant. 'If I have to evict you from here, you'll be lucky to find a room in a rookery!'

'I said I have your money.' Irritation crept into Law's voice. He shook Lady Avery's coin purse above his open palm and three solid coins tumbled out. He offered them to Tillmann and the landlord swept them away without hesitation. 'Perhaps you can use this to fix the door,' Law suggested.

'You're too far in arrears to be making demands, boy,' he said with one last distasteful look around the room. 'Where'd you get this coin anyway, hmm? I don't want to hear that it's been stolen, or that you've swindled some poor gent out of his weekly wage.'

'Then don't ask. Good day, Mr Tillman.' Law stepped forward, forcing Tillmann to retreat from the threshold. He closed the door in the sour man's face, latching the bolt. Tillmann's grumbling continued as he walked away, his cane clicking over the cobbled road.

With a groan, Law pressed his forehead to the door. He'd needed that coin. His pantry was empty; the bread he'd swiped from the Bucket was so far past stale it was growing mould and only good for kindling the hearth. He shouldn't have pissed off Briar—she was more likely to *close* his tab than settle it now.

But Lady Avery had money. Money he was sure she'd part with if he could provide her with closure on Camelia's disappearance. So what if it wasn't his usual business? If it paid his bills, what did it matter if he hunted man or monster? He couldn't afford to be picky—not with Briar currently showing him her thorns.

Kicking off his shoes, Law made his way back to the journals he'd retrieved from the wine cellar and took a seat. The records were extensive—Briar was thorough, after all. He opened the first folder.

'Copperton Chronicle. *Fourth Day, Ruby 7, 1182,*' Law read aloud as he picked up the torn newspaper article from late spring. '*Avery heiress missing.*'

He traced his finger down the page as he skimmed. '*Lady Cadance Avery, Miss Camelia's mother, remains hopeful but fears for her daughter's wellbeing. "I just want her home," Lady Avery told* The Chronicle, *offering a reward for those who come forward with information regarding her daughter's whereabouts.*

'*Preliminary investigations by the Crown Order found no signs of forced entry at the Avery Estate and suggest this may be the actions of a headstrong young runaway.*'

Law scoffed; he'd find nothing of use in the town circular. Gossip and speculation more than anything else. He leafed through the remaining contents—more articles from *The Chronicle* over the last three months, each briefer than the one before, with the final publication being a smudged portrait of Camelia with the word MISSING printed in block letters above her head. Law pulled it free of the bundle and set it aside with the etching of the Averys published alongside the first article.

'She closed the case but not her interest in it,' Law said curiously, noting how Briar continued to collect information on the missing girl long after she declared it a human crime. It was certainly an odd case, if not just for the attention it received in the papers. People disappeared all the time in Copperton with little more than a flyer on the town noticeboard. How much money did the Averys truly have? Repeated print run, a Crown Order investigation and now more *unorthodox* methods.

'Should press for more coin,' Law grumbled bitterly to himself and took the next document off the pile—Briar's journal. He recognised it immediately from her delicate hand on the cover: *The Avery Incident.*

'Sixthday, Ruby 9, 1182,' Law began. *'Avery Estate, back field. Camelia often plays in the copse beyond the fence. Last seen heading towards it, four days ago on Secondday, Ruby 5. The copse itself is unremarkable. Hawthorn present but uninhabited. No recent* sidhe *activity in the region.*

Law paused and looked up from his reading as Black Cat leapt onto the windowsill, limp pigeon clamped in her jaw.

'Brought your own food for once,' Law said, reaching out to scratch the feline's chin. She dropped the bird and nuzzled into his palm, chest rumbling. 'Care to share?'

The cat hissed; Law laughed. 'I'll find something later, then.'

Despite Black Cat's possessiveness of her meal, she did not eat, and instead sat on the table beside the books and watched Law with a slow blinking stare.

'Know anything about a faerie ring at the Avery estate?' he asked. 'No? Me neither.'

He returned to Briar's journal.

'Fire had been concealed beneath some rocks. Animal bones amongst the ashes—a rabbit, perhaps. Maybe a cat, or small dog.'

Black Cat chirruped. Law flicked forward a few pages.

'Winston Avery remains taciturn; Cadance insists this is his usual demeanour. He seeks to dismiss my service. Believes Camelia is gone and will leave it to the Crown Order to find the human perpetrators, if there are any. I am wont to agree with him.'

'So is old man Avery just a sceptic?' Law pondered aloud, scratching Black Cat's ear. 'Or did he have his own reasons for wanting Briar off the case?' He closed the journal and placed it back on the stack. It was half-four, according to his pocket watch. If he slept now, he'd be well rested for his investigation.

'C'mon, Cat,' he said, heading for the bedroom. 'Guess we'll find our answers tonight.'

CLOUDS COVERED THE MOON—THE perfect night for prowling. Law crouched in the garden, behind a tangle of overgrown roses, and waited for the light to be extinguished in the topmost room of the turret. He pulled out his pocket watch, tried to catch a glimpse of the face in the reflected light to no avail. It'd been after eleven when he'd set out from the Chamberpots; on a midweek day like Thirdsday, the working class were well and truly abed in preparation to rise with the sun. Some might have been at the Bucket—or perhaps even the

Marinelle—but they would have been too full of booze to pay mind to anyone else walking the streets.

Not that anyone saw him.

Anxiety trickled down Law's spine with each passing minute. It had been years since he last worked a stakeout—a hunting shack in a village outside of Copperton where a vampyr had taken up residence. She'd once been a young noble from Sunscourt by the look of her: blonde hair, golden eyes, which shone brightly with the cursed venom coursing through her veins. She'd begged for her life, as the humanoids always did, but still he shot her with a silver pellet. Briar had railed at him for that.

'Decapitation is the most effective means of felling a vampyr,' she'd chastised. 'Silver is for *emergencies*. Do you have any idea how much those pellets cost to make?'

Law never admitted she'd got the jump on him. That she'd had him pinned to the ground when he faltered at the sight of her blood-tears. He'd never seen a vampyr cry before. That meant she still had feelings—or she'd just been good at pretending.

Maybe Law had more in common with his prey than he thought.

The light flickered out in the upstairs window; Law's pulse jumped to life.

He waited another ten minutes before approaching the house, footsteps as sure and silent as a cat. Pulling on his gloves, he reached for the handle, giving it a little jiggle. Law frowned. Lady Avery was supposed to have left the door unlocked. An inconvenience, but not a dealbreaker.

He took out his lock picks. He was not in the habit of prowling properties uninvited, but he'd learnt the hard way it was better to have them and not need them than to be caught without.

Twice in one day.

It was a simple lock—much the same as the one on the wine cellar—and it clicked open with little more than a whisper. He kept a firm grip on the edge of the door, controlling its swing in case the hinges decided to creak. They didn't, and Law closed the door behind him, breath held in his lungs.

As his eyes adjusted to the new dark, he drew a mental map of the house. The parlour where he'd spoken with Lady Avery was to his right, and a grand staircase stood before him, winding up to the higher levels. From what he knew of such manors, the kitchen, dining room and wash closet would be on this level, beyond the staircase. Nothing of use down here—he'd need to find the girl's bedchamber, or Lord Avery's study.

If no supernatural forces were at play, then Winston Avery was the prime subject. He was suspicious in a way that made the Crown Order's lack of charges appear lazy or incompetent. Had old Winston paid them off?

Law eased himself up the stairs, gloved hand ghosting the handrail. The house was deathly silent, as was the night outside. Silent *and* dark. He could barely see to put one foot in front of the other. Once he was inside the girl's room he'd light his lantern, but here in the corridors, where light and shadows crept beneath doors, he was forced to paw around blindly.

The first door he passed was slightly ajar. Law stilled his lungs and opened his ears. Deep, steady breathing sounded within—the sound of sleep. There were two distinct patterns, one louder and punctuated with a nasally snore.

A drinker? Law mused as he backed away from the room. Lord Winston wouldn't be the first troubled man to drink himself to sleep. Relief loosened his muscles; a drunk sleeper was harder to rouse.

Emboldened by this assumption, Law continued down the hall, poking his head in half-open doorways until he reached one that was locked.

This must be Camelia's room.

He took out his lock picks and it gave way as easily as the front door. Inside, the room was cold. The window was sealed, the curtains drawn tight, and there was an old musty smell about the cramped space. Law opened the hinged glass eye of the lantern at his belt, lowered the wick to its smallest height, and lit it with his tinderbox. The warm orange glow of the short flame provided just enough light for Law to see around the room, but likely wouldn't penetrate the thick blinds to alert anyone who may be passing by on the street below.

The decor was everything Law expected of a young girl's room: a floral quilt with lace trim adorned the bed, complete with frilled throw pillows; a porcelain doll with pearlescent black eyes stared at Law from its place atop them. A cold chill ran through his body. Why did the wealthy insist on capturing the likeness of children in pale faced dolls? What was wrong with the rag and wool approximations the commonfolk favoured?

Despite having a place of honour on the girl's bed, it didn't appear well-loved. Not a strand of hair was out of place, and the layer of dust shining dully in the lamplight suggested neglect that spanned beyond Camelia's four-month disappearance. The room itself looked staged—unloved even. Not the room of a child who left on an ordinary day with every intent to return.

Or someone who left in a hurry.

Law stepped around the bed towards the writing desk. It was the same layout as his dorm room at the academy in Verredeen: bed by the door, desk under the window and very little else. The feminine touches were an obvious attempt by her mother to make the space seem homely, but it had all the warmth of a barren study hall.

Some childhood, Law mused as ran a finger across the edge of the writing table. *No wonder she loved playing in the field.* Lady Avery had described her daughter as quiet and withdrawn; perhaps a diary could reveal what her parents themselves could not.

The door slammed shut. Law hit the floor as a silently as haste would allow. He extinguished the lantern and tucked his knees up tight and small against his chest to hide in the shadow of the bed. His breath plumed in a cloud before his face. The temperature dropped to frigid.

Spirit activity.

Law's pulse flickered. Whatever it was that tied Camelia's spirit to this house, he'd just infringed upon it. Something in the writing table? Something secret?

Something important.

For a spirit to guard it so intently, it must hold the answers to her disappearance. But if Law forced his way into that drawer there was no telling what she'd do—to him *or* her family.

'It's happening again!' Lady Avery, from down the hall, her voice crackling with fear. 'It's her!'

'Enough of this, woman,' a man growled groggily in response. 'I opened the window upstairs when I was smoking my cigars. Wind must've blown the door shut.'

The outside air was as still as gravestones.

The conversation descended into inaudible mumbles before fading into silence. A slight smile tugged at the corner of Law's mouth as his esteem of Lady Avery grew. Her forced, hysterical performance irritated her husband into dismissing her fears. Nothing from his earlier meeting with her suggested she was afraid of the spirit in her home; she just wanted answers. Justice for her daughter. Did she suspect her husband as well?

Satisfied the Averys would not leave their bed, Law picked himself up, swallowing a groan from joints gone stiff in stillness and cold. The spirit still hung heavily about the room. He reached into the breast pocket of his jacket and took out a small leather book no larger than a cigarillo case. It was thick and battered, the text so small even Law with his strong eyesight needed to squint to make out the letters in the dim light.

'Expel, expel...' he whispered aloud as he flicked through the pages. It had been a long time since he'd needed to exorcise a poltergeist and Briar's book of incantations, which had been added to over the years, had no logical order. Once he found what he was looking for, he pitched his voice as loud as he dared and commanded, '*Contremiscite et fugite!*'

A sharp *whoosh* swept through the room, billowing the curtains despite the window being shut tight. The 'tremble and flea' incantation may not send the spirit beyond the Veil, but it would see it returned to its corpse.

To the Taschenwilde.

Law stood frozen for a moment, waiting for footsteps of alarm from down the hall. Silence prevailed. He edged towards the dresser, tugged on the drawer and found it locked. But before a frustrated groan could tumble from his lips, he spied an open jewellery box, its metallic contents catching the light of his lantern. He leant over the table for a closer look. Some copper coins, a ring or two, a locket on a delicate chain—and a key.

The drawer opened without protest. It was stuffed to near-bursting with books and loose sheets of paper filled with the musings of a young girl. Law picked up the first of many journals and brought it under his meagre light to read.

'*Elor Must Fall,*' Law whispered the title aloud. Not a journal but a book—one he'd seen before, along time ago, during his brief, ill-fated stint at the academy. The book, which was decisively short—no wider than his thumb—systematically tore apart the Church of Elor by debunking its teachings of The One God as being a fictitious creation of its founding members. Churches all over Dallalmar had been sacked, priests driven from their homes, and landholders, who had long paid stipends to the clergy, rioted through the streets. Worship of Elor had all but been outlawed by Sunscourt since, though many of the elderly still muttered nighttime prayers before bed. What on earth was a thirteen-year-old girl doing with a copy of it?

Law set the book aside and reached for what he was sure was a diary. It bulged with folded loose letters that scattered across the desk as he opened it to read. It fell naturally towards the most recent entries, dated one month before Camelia's disappearance.

Pearl 23, 1182. Father said I'm one of the best candidates. Tomorrow, we'll meet the gods. If I'm chosen, Father says I'll have to go away for a while. I don't mind. I'm ready.

'Ready for what?' Law flicked to the next page.

Pearl 25, 1182. There were six other girls at the audience. I don't know where they took us because we were blindfolded. We weren't to see the gods—not until we were chosen to do so. Most of the girls were afraid. I wasn't. Father told me to be brave. To be strong. And I was. I was the best of them all. I didn't tremble when the god approached me. Not even when he kissed my neck—

'What kind of sick fuck—'

—and let out a sharp little squeal, kind of like a pig. It was very strange and not what I expected at all. I don't mean to speak ill of the gods, but it smelled terribly. Like mud and mould and wet dog hair. Or maybe that was one of the girls. Someone said she was a farmer's daughter.

I've felt ... odd since I came back home. Something squirms inside my belly, like I've swallowed a worm. Mother thinks I've taken ill, especially since I've been wearing a scarf indoors. The god's kiss left a horrid red ring on my neck, raw and raised like a burn.

Law's hand went instinctively to his own neck, fingers circling the puckered wound. His heart was beating so loud he was sure the Averys would hear it, and when he turned the page to the last entry, it practically burst from his chest.

The double-page spread was covered in rough, repeating sketches of the nine-sided shape with its irregular star enclosed within. The book tumbled from Law's grip and landed on the table with a hollow thud. He shoved his first in his mouth, biting down hard to contain his curses. He felt sick to his core. It took several deep breaths to regain his composure, and even then, a slight tremor crept into his hand. He tucked the diary into his jacket, swept the rest of the displaced papers back into the drawer, locked it and returned the key to its place in the jewellery box.

Skin prickled with goose flesh, Law slipped out of the Avery estate with more questions than answers following him home.

5

CAIT SIDHE

Law sat in his tub, sucking on his fourth cigarillo. Smoke filled his narrow home despite the open window and left the corners of his vision white with haze. He slumped low in the bath, an ache forming in the small of his back from the poor angle and support; his arse had long since gone numb.

Camelia's diary lay on the table, open to the horrific collage of dark stars. He'd been quick to shuck his boots and coat, both of which lay in a crumpled heap beside the tub, where he sat soaking by the hearth fire. Something about cleaning his body cleaned his thoughts too, and he could contemplate the evidence a little more now.

Winston Avery had lured his daughter into a cult. Camelia herself confirmed that, even if she was too young to realise what was happening. How many other girls had gone missing at the hands of some wretched bastard claiming to be a god?

Law sucked in a long drag and held the smoke deep in his lungs, a hand massaging the wound on his neck.

'Mud and wet dog,' he muttered around the cigarillo between his lips. Had the creature in the forest smelt like that? It had certainly reeked, but the stench of mold and peat were hardly unusual in a place as dark and damp as the Taschenwilde. Could it—

Law startled as Black Cat jumped through the window, breaking his bleary-eyed stare on the diary. The feline visitor sat down on the table and commenced washing herself, rolling a paw over each ear.

'Someone else feed you today?' Law asked through a cloud of exhaled smoke. Her content grooming could only mean one thing: a full belly.

Black Cat chirruped briefly then proceeded to lick her anus. Law scoffed in affront and leant his head back over the rim of the tub, chin pointing towards the ceiling and eyes rolling closed. His fingertip circled the bite, still tender and swollen. Was something growing inside his body? Something wicked and grotesque, waiting to tear its way free? He wanted to talk it through with Briar, but she'd dismiss him the moment he opened his mouth.

None of our business, she'd said of the nine-sided symbol.

But she knew, Law realised, eyes snapping open to the cobwebs dangling from the exposed rafters. *She'd seen that symbol before—at the Avery estate.*

'The alchemist knows more than she's telling you.'

The feminine voice almost sent Law tumbling from the tub. He reached for the pistol amongst his discarded clothes as he floundered, levelling the barrel in the direction of the window as he straightened.

A woman sat on the table where Black Cat had groomed—naked, save for the long dark hair draped across her breasts. A silver streak parted the black curtain hanging over her right shoulder, colourless like the pearlescent, slitted eyes that blinked twice then assumed a normal shape and pale blue hue.

The naked woman raised her palms. 'I'm just the messenger.'

'Whose messenger?' Law demanded gruffly.

The woman lowered her hands, shoulders relaxing to a slight slump. 'Now where'd be the fun in that?' She unfurled from her bunched position on the table. Slowly, but without any conscious attempt at seduction. Despite her youthful appearance, there was an air of maturity about her, and Law didn't doubt for a second she'd lived well beyond *his* years.

'You can lower that weapon; I mean you no harm,' she said, tucking the white streak of hair behind her ear, which pinched to a subtle tip.

'I'm good, thanks,' Law said flatly. Sweat began to tickle his palm despite the icy water about his hips. 'So that's your hawthorn tree, then?'

'I've been known to look in on it from time to time. But no, it's not *mine*. I'm a wanderer. You know that, because you know me. We've shared a bed, after all.'

Black Cat.

Law relaxed his grip on the pistol ever so slightly. 'You're a *cait sidhe.*'

A feline grin split her face. 'And you can call me Cait. I don't mind.'

He lowered his gun, accepting she was no immediate threat, but not yet prepared to holster it entirely. His skin crawled at his ignorance. He'd been thinking aloud to this cat for months. Had she reported it all back to whatever master she served?

'How've you avoided Briar's attention all this time?'

'Nothing's more invisible than a beggar, and that includes the four-legged kind,' she said with a wry little smile on her full red lips. 'There's nothing suspicious about a stray cat, Mr Reed—yes, yes, I know your name, don't look so surprised. You're not as mysterious as you think you are.'

'What do you want?' Water splashed as Law stepped out of the tub, as naked as his guest. He set the pistol down as he reached for the towel hung over the back of the chair, gaze never leaving the *cait sidhe*'s face.

'I'm hungry,' she said.

Law snorted, sluicing the water from his lower body then wrapping the towel around his hips. 'You still expect me to cook for you when you have two hands to do it yourself?'

Cait shook her head, the tangle of long hair swaying with her breasts. 'Not for food—for a soul.'

Law reached for his pistol.

'Wait—*wait*. Not for *your* soul,' Cait clarified, hands stretched out as if they could shield her from a bullet. 'A dead one. From a body not yet buried.' Her predatory smile stretched. 'Do you know where I might find one?'

She knew about the girl in the Taschenwilde; Black Cat had been here when he returned, that foetal abomination in tow. The cat had hissed and growled at it, alerting Law to the fact it still *moved*.

'You saw what I found in the forest alongside that body. Seemed to me you didn't much care for it. What do you know?'

'Nothing yet.' Cait shrugged, swinging her legs back and forth beneath the table like a child. 'But let me eat her soul, and I'll find out.'

Law hesitated. The girl deserved a proper burial every bit as much as Lady Avery deserved closure—and a way to remember her daughter. But with her soul already restless and latching onto her possessions, he couldn't allow any sentimental mementos to remain. Souls turned savage the longer they were kept from the Veil. He'd sent it back to her corpse once, and leaving a part of her behind might cause it to go wandering again. If the *cait sidhe* were to eat it...

'What happens to the soul once you're done with it?' Law asked, waving the pistol as he spoke.

'What happens to the air once we breathe it?' she countered, then took in a deep breath, held it, and released. 'Our bodies extract what we need and expel the rest.'

'And what is it that you need?'

'Memories, mostly. And magic,' Cait added as an afterthought. 'Shifting between forms certainly does use a lot of it.'

There was countless lore surrounding souls, much of it conflicting. If faerie deemed it magic, Law was not going to argue—about *that*, anyway.

'Bodies drop by the dozen in this town,' he pressed. 'Why that girl? Why go prowling through the Taschenwilde for a corpse when you could just wait outside the undertakers?'

Cait slipped off the table and stalked towards him on impossibly light feet. She was tall and lithe, all muscle and sinew, her nakedness revealing curves otherwise hidden beneath clothes. Law kept his eyes—and his pistol—locked on her face.

'You want Lady Avery's coin purse, don't you?' she challenged, breath hot on Law's cheeks. 'You want closure for her. And for yourself.'

'And why do you care about that?'

A dry smile curled the corners of the *cait sidhe*'s lips. 'What's happened in your life that's made you sceptical of kindness?'

'Spent too long in Copperton.'

Her grin broadened and she expelled a little burst of air that may have been a laugh. 'And yet you took in a stray. Gave it food from your own plate.'

'Cats aren't people,' Law said pointedly.

'Neither am I.'

Her words cut his better judgement, slipping through the cracks to where he almost felt trust. But faerie folk were to be left alone, not befriended or hunted—not unless they became a problem. Even then, investigators had been known to turn a blind eye.

Law swallowed and set his pistol back down on the chair. He took a cigarillo from its case—the last one had fallen in the bath from the shock of the *cait sidhe*'s appearance—balanced it between his lips as he lit it and took a long, long drag. Slowly, he expelled the smoke in the *cait sidhe*'s face. She did not even blink.

'You're going to need some clothes,' Law said evenly.

A delighted smile curled the woman's lips. 'I look good in blue.'

MEREDITH SET OUT TEA and cake for Law and Lady Avery before excusing herself from the room with a wordless bow. The door closed with a gentle click and a moment passed before either of them started speaking.

'I trust last night was successful?' Lady Avery asked, vigorously stirring a cube of sugar into her tea. 'I'd hate to think I let you traipse around my home on a whim.'

'I have a lead,' Law confirmed.

'I'm not paying you for *leads*. You promised answers!'

Law sat a moment to choose his next words. There were dark rings beneath Lady Avery's eyes that her powders did little to disguise. Had something else troubled her last night? Law had left not long after she'd woken and assumed she'd gone back to sleep. Would she welcome confirmation of her daughter's passing—or would it loosen whatever threads currently held her together?

'Camelia will be at rest soon,' he said, telling Lady Avery what she needed to hear without bluntly stating that her little girl was dead.

Avery paused, the teacup but a hair's breadth from her mouth. Her hand trembled, so did her lips, and the moisture welling in her eyes highlighted the redness around the edges. She set the cup down, sniffed, and regained her composure by pouring Law a cup of tea he really didn't want.

'Tomorrow morning,' he said, watching steam drift off the brew, 'go to the girl's room. Burn whatever is in her writing drawer. It's anchoring her spirit to this house; you'll need to burn it to let her go.'

'And her body?' Lady Avery's voice cracked despite her best efforts.

'...won't be coming home. I'm sorry. It's ... not a sight any mother should see.'

He let her digest that difficult truth while he thought how best to raise his second order of business. He'd left the *cait sidhe* in his house, naked but for the bedsheet draped around her. The thought of it twisted his gut. Law never entertained guests in his home—female or otherwise—and the thought of someone alone in his private space set him at ill-ease. He had no valuables the *cait sidhe* could steal, if the creature was wont to commit such mischief, and yet he still felt vulnerable.

'Try the cake,' Lady Avery insisted. 'It was Camelia's favourite.' She speared her own portion with a delicate fork and popped it into her mouth.

Law pulled the plate closer to him, gave it a sniff. It was some sort of sponge, layered with berry jam and cream, and dusted with powdered sugar. It did not excite him. Law would've much preferred a savoury snack—something stodgy and thick with pork grease—but he was not in any position to turn down food, dead girl's favourite or otherwise. And so he took a bite, and then two, pleased to find it not as cloyingly sweet as it looked.

'It's good,' Law said. It wasn't a lie; he finished the whole slice and washed it down with the cooling tea. *That* was a mistake, but he tried not to let the grimace show on his face as he swallowed. 'I appreciate your hospitality. I wish I could have brought you better news about your daughter.'

'You told me nothing I didn't already know, Mr Reed,' she said softly and set her fork down on the empty plate, tines pointed politely at twelve o'clock. 'How did she die? You must know that at least. Tell me: why can't bury my little girl?'

Law scraped the remaining crumbs and dollops of cream up on his fork to delay answering. He couldn't tell her the truth—not it its entirety. How do you tell a grieving mother her husband's the one responsible? It would be kinder to lie.

'She was found in the Taschenwilde,' he said, eyes on plate. 'When you spoke of how she liked to explore the estate, I thought she may have grown bold enough to wander further afield. She hadn't gotten far, but it seems she fell and broke her leg.'

Lady Avery sucked in a gasp, covering her mouth with her hands as tears formed in her eyes. He'd said enough; her imagination would fill in the rest.

'There's one more thing I must ask,' Law said quickly, before she succumbed to her grief and sent him away. 'A rather odd request, I'm afraid. But it will bring Camelia peace.'

With a napkin, Lady Avery dabbed the inner corners of her eyes and sniffed away her sobs. 'What is it?'

'I need an old dress of yours.' When Lady Avery flushed with affront, Law hastily added, 'To wrap the body as I cremate it—to stop the haunting. I've sent the soul back to her body, but unless she is put to rest, it will find its way back here. Let me bring something of home to her. Something special and familiar.'

The frazzled woman nodded slowly. 'Yes ... yes, of course. She would want to feel close to us again. I'll have Meredith fetch a gown for her at once.'

Lady Avery summoned her housemaid to do just that and the two of them sat in an unpleasant silence while they awaited her return. Law itched for a cigarillo. He scanned the room for an ashtray; there were none. He tried swallowing saliva to distract himself.

When Meredith returned, she handed Law a large garment box and showed him to the door.

'When you're up to it, clear out her room,' Law told Lady Avery from the threshold. 'Putting things away helps process the loss. That's what my mother said, when my sister died.'

Heat rose to his cheeks at having shared a piece of himself, but she just nodded absently and said nothing. Law was about to raise the question of payment when Meredith shut the door in his face, ending any chance of negotiating his compensation.

There'll be a better time for that, he thought bitterly as trudged back into town, stomach rumbling and box growing heavy in his arms. He should have specified a nightgown for Camelia's burial shroud—not whatever gaudy abomination lay nestled in this box. He didn't much care what the *cait sidhe* dressed herself in so long as she didn't follow him across town completely nude or in men's garments—though in Copperton, it was hard to tell which was more scandalous.

Law found the door latched when he arrived home and was grateful the creature'd had enough sense to lock up if she'd decided to flee. A part of him hoped she *had* gone—though that would leave him with the awkward predicament of discarding a woman's dress. But Cait was right where he'd left her, sitting on the foot of his bed.

'This will have to do,' Law said, setting the garment box on the table. Cait stood eagerly, sheet dropping from her shoulders, and trotted over to inspect the gift. She tore into like a child with a bag of boiled lollies and held up a silk taffeta gown of pale blue. The bodice was stiff with a boned corset, and the skirt voluminous with petticoats of horsehair.

No wonder it weighed so much.

Cait stared at him incredulously. 'There're no undergarments.'

'You'll have to go without.' He was not about to go back and ask a well-to-do lady for a pair of her unmentionables—not if he wanted to get *paid*.

'Mr Reed, are you suggesting I traipse through the Taschenwilde without any drawers under this fancy dress of mine?' Despite the scandal in her tone, mischief shone bright behind those feline eyes.

'I'm suggesting you turn back into a cat.'

'And give up wearing this pretty thing? Absolutely not!'

Law scoffed and turned his back while she dressed. She hadn't asked, but it seemed the proper thing to do, even though she chuckled at his expense. It wasn't that she made him uncomfortable, he just really would have preferred she stayed a cat. Last time he checked, animals didn't talk.

'Excuse me, kind sir, could I trouble you to help with my buttons?' she asked with a mocking lilt. 'Don't worry, my breasts are firmly tucked away!'

Law turned to find her back to him, long hair pulled forward over her shoulders as she clutched the dress against her chest. Swallowing the urge to grumble a retort, Law did as he was asked, his thick fingers fighting with the stiff, delicate buttons. Why choose such a lavish and impractical gown to be burned with a corpse? Law'd pictured something old and soft and simple, like a sentimental cotton shift. Perhaps this was a mother's way of saying goodbye—a fancy dress in place of a parting kiss.

'Done,' Law said, fixing the last button at the base of Cait's spine. She spun to face him, hair whipping as she plumped the fullskirt in all its grandeur.

'Oh, it is *good* to be a woman again!' She cackled with glee, twirling side to side like a little girl. 'No shoes?' Her expression fell as she double-checked the box.

'I didn't go shopping at a boutique,' Law snapped. 'I'll find you some old woollen socks.'

Cait flapped her hand. 'Not to worry; I like being barefoot. Well, come along then. My belly's proper rumbling and I'd like to get this soul before it spoils further. Are you with me, Mr Reed? Or would you rather Copperton gossips about seeing you take a fancy young lady into the Taschenwilde after dark?'

That was the last thing Law needed. Investigators were maligned enough without rumours of him being a pervert or debaucher spreading through town; the less he did to evoke the ire of the commonfolk, the better.

'I'll pack what I need to bury the girl in travel luggage,' he said, and went into the adjoining room to pull a battered leather trunk out from beneath his bed. It had seen better days—and many, many more in storage—but was large enough to accommodate a lady's wardrobe essentials, as befitting their charade.

It'd also fit a spade.

'Wait here,' Law instructed and left via the front door. At the back of his cottage was a narrow shed filled with tools the previous tenant had left behind. Whoever it had been must have fancied themselves a gardener and attempted to cultivate *something* on the dry strip of earth behind the Chamberpots. Skeletons of long departed shrubberies poked through autumn leaves, now thicker than the soles of Law's well-loved boots.

He pried open the busted door with the same brutality required to enter his home. The spade was his—burying bodies or exhuming graves was a key requirement of his profession—but the rest he'd inherited. Much of it was rusted beyond worth, but with an extra body to protect in the Taschenwilde, it wouldn't hurt to be prepared.

Law picked up a small hand sickle. He scraped his thumb on the nicked and pocked steel and found its edge sufficiently sharp. Not the most refined weapon, but it would serve in close quarters—or if he ran out of ammunition.

Back inside, he placed the spade and sickle inside the trunk along with a sack of salt and bottle of oil from his larder. Cait peered around the doorframe, eyebrows high on her forehead as he buckled the straps tight.

'That's an odd assortment of things you got there,' she said mildly. 'And a cumbersome pack to be lugging through the woods.'

'I'm a bodyguard hired to escort you along the old highway to meet a coachman who'll take you the rest of the way to Sunscourt,' Law explained. No one was likely to stop them for conversation so they had to *look* like that was the only explanation for their travels.

'Plan on doing a wee bit of cooking on the road then?' She gestured towards the salt and oil.

'For the body,' he said. 'To cleanse her soul so she can find rest.'

'I'm going to eat her soul.'

The words were so matter of fact they gave Law pause. He'd been so eager to latch on to a solution for all his unanswered questions, he hadn't really sat down and thought about what it meant. If the *cait sidhe* ate her soul, would it be any different to condemning her to the Otherworld—the antithesis of the peace found beyond the Veil?

He'd best not think about that.

Law tightened the trunk's buckles once more, brushed off the knees of his pants, and stood back to full height. 'So *I* can find rest, then,' he conceded with a sigh. 'Come. We should be on the road before dark.'

6

CORPSE RAIDERS

CAIT TRAVERSED THE THICK undergrowth of the Taschenwilde with unlikely grace. Despite her bare feet and voluminous skirts, she kept pace with Law, stepping over fallen trees, tangles of vines and slippery, moss-covered rocks with all the agility of a cat.

Having entered the wood from the old road to maintain their charade, it was a much longer journey to the clearing where Law had found the girl's body. They lost close to two hours looping back along the perimeter to find the tracks he had followed a week prior. It was no easy task: the footsteps had faded, obscured by fallen leaves and the moist, malleable ground. Law led the way with his lantern, then knelt to inspect scuffs on a boulder obscured by the undergrowth. Made by his own boots, it seemed, judging by the tread. Yet this strip of forest hardly looked familiar. Every path was very much the same—dark and rotten yet filled with life. The air was thick with a presence he felt but never saw—a prickle always on the back of his neck. Uneasiness curled in his belly. Scratched at his skin. Stiffened his joints. The desire to flee swelled with every breath.

'You're awfully sensitive to ley lines,' Cait observed.

Law looked back over his shoulder as he stood. 'What?'

She tipped her head towards him, gesturing at the sweat beading on his forehead. At the hasty rise and fall of his chest. 'Must have a touch of *waerloga* in you.'

'*What?*'

She chuckled, twirling the ends of her long hair around her fingers. 'Never mind,' she said, a cryptic smile on her lips. 'The ley line is very active tonight; maybe even those closed to magic can feel its vibrations.'

Was that what it was? Law had been in the Taschenwilde a score of times and never felt the dread and discomfort that had come over him since discovering Camelia and that foetus. He wiped the sweat off his brow with his forearm and took long, slow breaths to calm the anxious buzz in his chest.

'I do hope the body's not too much farther,' Cait mused and rocked back on her heels. 'It's not wise to linger when the ley line's in such a state.'

'It's not wise to linger here at all,' Law mumbled, reattaching the lantern to his belt. He hoisted the cumbersome trunk up over his shoulder, letting it clap against his scapula as they trudged deeper into the wood. He was sure they were close now. They only need walk straight until—

Law raised his fist; Cait halted behind him. Carefully, Law set the trunk down, quiet as a whisper, and pulled his pistol from its holster on his thigh. He took a step forward. Then two, edging closer to the break in the trees where the girl's body had been found. Cait followed, moving slowly to mute the rustle of her skirts. A wet snaffle came through the mist. Thick and sloppy, punctuated with tearing muscle and crunching bone. Law cocked his pistol.

The bullet ripped through the trees with a thunderous clap. It found purchase in a meaty body and the squeal of a speared pig broke the stillness. In the chaos of scattering feet, Law kicked the trunk back towards Cait.

'Arm yourself!' he shouted, reloading the barrel. 'We've got ghouls.'

'*Ghouls*?' The *cait sidhe*'s voice was incredulous in a way Law thought impossible for an immortal being. Face pale and eyes wide, she pulled the hand sickle from the trunk and held it in a loose grip.

'Corpse raiders—usually found in cemeteries,' Law explained. He edged into the clearing, pistol loaded and waiting. 'They feed on the flesh of the dead.'

Something moved in his peripheral vision; he fired another shot into the darkness. An unnatural laugh cackled through the trees. He needed more light.

Law unhooked the lantern from his belt and tossed it into the clearing where the girl's corpse had been. The glass eye shattered and the oil from the fuel tank spilled onto the leaf litter, flames moving with liquid grace.

'What the fuck are you doing!?' Cait shrieked. 'You'll set the whole forest ablaze!'

'It's far too damp for that,' Law said through gritted teeth. He closed one eye and focussed on the slippery shadow pacing behind the tree line. 'It'll die once it burns through the oil. Got you, you foul fuck.'

The pistol shot cracked through the night.

The beast tumbled into view as it died, a bloody crater in its skull from his bullet. Its thick grey skin was pimpled with warts like a toad, and a potbelly protruded grotesquely from an otherwise skeletal frame. It was hairless and naked, somewhere between a beast and a man with long, clawed hands and feet. A ribbon of papery dead flesh was caught between its sharp crooked teeth.

'There're more out there,' Law said, lowering his pistol as he stepped towards the dead ghoul. 'But I think I've scared them off. They're not all that fond of fire.'

'Few of us are.'

Cait relaxed her arm, sickle slipping from her loose grip. It dropped into the grass at Law's feet as she eased past him towards the corpse the ghouls had been feeding on. Fire crackled in the oil spill and embers scattered into the black sky, illuminating the clearing like a hearth.

It was unmistakably the girl. The remaining abdominal cavity had been eaten away, stripped down to the skeletal framework of her pelvis, spine and ribs. Law sucked in a deep breath through his mouth as he approached, squatting down beside her to sweep the brittle remains of her blonde hair aside with the barrel of his pistol.

A round scar, purple and puckered, rose from the grey skin of her neck.

'Camelia Avery,' Law whispered. He rubbed his free hand down his face. His fingers found the mark on his own neck and lingered there a moment too long.

'It's not the same,' the *cait sidhe* said.

Law whipped round to face her. 'What?'

'It's not the same. The mark on your neck. It's not like hers.'

'How do you know?'

'Because she smelt *dead* when she left with them—the men who took her away from Avery estate.'

'You *saw* them? What did they do with her? Where did they go?'

'Let me eat her soul and find out,' Cait insisted, eagerness uncomfortably present in her voice. Her hands trembled like a drunk too long without liquor as she hunched down on all fours. She stalked up the body, straddling the corpse like a spider wrapping prey in a web. With a crack, her jaw unhinged and opened unnaturally wide. Her eyes rolled back in her skull until only white remained.

She was ... feeding. It was sick—grotesque, even—but Law could not look away. His skin crawled as a stream of silver smoke rose from the corpse and into the *cait sidhe*'s open maw. Law forced himself to turn his back, vision blurring as it took in the red glow of the fire. He blinked twice and then rubbed his eyes. Now the flames were dying, the shadows fell differently around the clearing, obscuring the dead ghoul. No. Not hidden—*gone*.

Law drew his pistol. 'Cait, we've got company,' he hissed; she didn't answer. 'Fuck.' He took two long strides, positioning himself between the fire and the feeding *cait sidhe*, back to the crackling oil in case the ghouls circled around to attack them from behind. Its meagre flames should deter them ... but then again, he'd been certain that ghoul was dead. Had the colony cannibalised its corpse?

Something flittered through the shadows; Law fired, missed. The ghouls' menacing laugh followed the echoing thunder-crack of the pistol. He checked his ammunition pouch; he was quickly running out of bullets.

Law reloaded, fumbling with the lead pellets as he attempted to stuff the barrel while keeping an eye on the tree line. Sweat trickled down his spine from the heat of the flames. Having burnt through the oil, it fought to catch the damp leaf litter and sent plumes of thick white smoke up into the air. With the *cait sidhe* all but in a trance, Law would have to keep the ghouls' attention on him. His best chance of doing that was to stay close to the fire—and keep it burning for as long as possible. How long did it take to eat a soul? Would his bullets last as long as the fuel? What if he ran out of both?

The trunk, Law recalled, gaze darting to where he'd dumped it outside the clearing. He'd packed oil for burning Camelia's body deep in the grave. The sickle was somewhere there, too. He would struggle to hit a target with all this smoke, but everything died once its head was cut off. Law hoped that held true for ghouls, too.

That haunting cackle echoed once again and sent a chill down Law's spine. A creature crawled from the undergrowth on all fours, as grey and bloated as a corpse. It was a juvenile, yet to harden into the lithe muscle that clung to a mature ghoul's skeletal frame. Like so many young, its teeth were needle-sharp and dripping with the viscous black blood of its kind.

So they really will *eat anything dead.*

Law instinctively took a step back and the heat from the fire sputtered up his legs. The thick wool of his trousers prevented him from going up in flames, but the sting served as a timely reminder he had nowhere to run.

Shit.

He raised his loaded pistol, levelled it at the beast and emptied the barrel into its head. It exploded like a melon under a mallet. A piercing shriek erupted from deep in the forest, but Cait did not even flinch. Law was reloading when a second ghoul burst from the darkness and launched itself at the vulnerable *cait sidhe*, clawed feet outstretched for the kill. Law sprang towards it, intercepting its attack with a bodily collision that knocked it off track. He landed heavily on his shoulder, upper arm scraping over a rock hidden beneath the leaves as he rolled back to his feet. He hissed, pain searing down his left arm. The iron tang of blood seeping through his torn sleeve sent the ghoul into a frenzy—and drew it Law's way. With the smouldering fire belching smoke as it struggled to live, he could barely make out the creature in front of him, let alone see what other dangers lay in wait. A shiver crawled across his flesh. He was so exposed. Even the forest seemed to close in around him.

'Alright, you fucker, let's go.' Law lowered his centre of gravity, knees soft and ready to evade if the creature pounced at him. The ghoul twitched and jerked, incensed by the smell of fresh blood. Erratic and unpredictable, it was the worst kind of target. He wouldn't be able to dodge forever, and in these close quarters, reloading while on the defence would be impossible without a distraction.

He needed the sickle. A retreat would open up distance between him and his target but without a lantern he'd be running blind through the darkness of the Taschenwilde. He could reload with muscle memory alone but what if it chose not to give chase and turned on Cait instead? Law clenched his fists. Was he prepared to take that risk?

I have no choice.

Slowly, Law edged away, gaze locked on the ghoul's distorted shape through the smoke. He could see its eyes and the intense connection triggered an animalistic challenge that made the beast snarl. Certain now it would give chase, Law turned and broke into a sprint. There was just enough light to see the flattened undergrowth they'd trampled through on their way to the clearing. The boxy shadow at the edge of visibility was probably the trunk—it had to be. He didn't have the luxury of being wrong.

The beast was gaining on him. It snapped like a hound on the hunt, moving faster on all fours than Law could run. The dark silhouette of the trunk came into view, and Law passed his eyes over the surroundings, hoping to catch a glint of steel among the leaves.

Sharp claws clipped his ankle mid-stride, knocking him off-balance. They slashed through the thick leather of his boot, but it did enough to protect his flesh from serious injury. He broke his fall with his forearms and used the momentum to roll to his back. His sweeping leg collided with something solid and the ghoul careened off into the undergrowth with a howl. Law groaned, winded, and struggled to rise.

The beast recovered faster.

Before Law could get to his feet, it pounced, pinning him to the ground. Its claws dug into his shoulders, abusing the wound already sustained from the earlier fall. Law thrashed under its grip, tried to shake it off. He drove his knees into its bulging stomach to no avail.

Its belly was hard like a stone and the impact hurt Law more than it seemed to harm the creature. Razor-sharp teeth snapped at his face. Law wedged an elbow against its throat to hold it back. It choked and gurgled but was stronger than its emaciated frame had any right to be. Soon, it would overpower him.

'Cait!' Law screamed as his free hand pawed through the mud and leaves for something to bludgeon himself free. His fingers danced over small rocks and sticks, and he settled on a fistful of grit to spray in the ghoul's bulbous eyes. The beast keened and shook its head, affording Law enough distraction to scramble a few inches free where he caught a glint of steel in the grass.

The sickle!

Law stretched as far as he could. His fingertips brushed the weapon, but it wasn't enough to gain purchase. The slick, muddy handle fell away as the ghoul once again snapped at his face. Law rammed his forearm into its open mouth. He screamed as its jaw clamped down, needle-teeth piercing leather and flesh. The unexpected thrust unbalanced the ghoul, affording Law the space to reach for the sickle. Blood pouring down his arm, he gripped the curved blade and swung it towards the ghoul. He hooked it right under the chin, tearing through its throat as he swept his arm away from his body. The nicked blade became wedged in the ghoul's vertebrae and Law had to strain to wrench it free, severing head from shoulders in the process. Muscles spasmed as it died, the jaw slackening as the creature fell limply atop Law, blood fountaining across his face and neck. He gagged and kicked the corpse aside, taking a moment to lie there on his back, drawing deep breaths into his lungs and scrubbing his sleeve over his eyes. If another beast fell upon him now, he was fucked, but he heard no footsteps prowling the perimeter; no more mocking, ghoulish laughter, echoing in the deep.

Finally, they were alone.

'Fuck this fucking forest,' Law cursed. His arm throbbed where the ghoul had bitten him, slashing right through the wounds he'd sustained from the broken glass only a few days before. He'd need to visit Briar after this—need to find out how best to treat a ghoul bite. Did they have venom? Any foulness he'd need to flush from his body? He supposed they did, feeding on carrion. His flesh crawled.

'Mr Reed?' Cait's hoarse, uncertain voice trembled through the trees; Law sat up.

'Over here,' he replied, unable to stop the groan that escaped his lips as he stood. Elor's fucking balls, he was too old for this shit.

Cait was sitting back on her heels, hands resting on her thighs, beside Camelia Avery's mangled body. Her bronze skin shone as if freshly varnished, a pearlescent sheen swirling beneath the surface. Her cat eyes sparkled.

'What happened to you?' she asked, raising one eyebrow as Law approached, red blood streaming down his right arm and ghoul ichor fouling his face and coat.

'Ghouls,' he said flatly.

'So much for scaring them off.'

Law let the barb hit without protest and squatted opposite Cait. He took a deep breath to steel himself before tuning his gaze upon Camelia's corpse. The ghouls had made a feast of her: the torso was stripped bare, and the meat of her legs had been devoured, leaving the bloated, black feet untouched. Her hands had also been spared and laid outstretched in the mud as she had died, scarred palms upturned.

'Have you seen this before?' Law asked, gesturing to the shrivelled nine-sided shape etched into the girl's skin. The *cait sidhe* didn't answer, her gaze distant and unfixed.

'*Cait.*'

'She wanted the child,' she said softly, eyes unfixed. 'She wanted it right up until it killed her. She was proud to have been chosen.'

Law's gut roiled. 'So, it was a child?'

No answer.

'Did someone impregnate that little girl? *Cait*?' He grabbed her arms to seize her attention. Flesh like hot metal, Law jerked away at the searing touch. The luminescence faded from her skin and eyes, and she turned to look at him, profound grief written across her face.

'Not in the way that you mean, no. I'm sorry, Mr Reed,' she said, voice thick with emotion as she choked out the words. 'Her soul was very damaged. I can't tell you anything more.'

'That's *it*?' Law snarled. 'All this was for *nothing*?'

'She knew what she was doing. This path was not forced upon her,' the *cait sidhe* shot back. 'She wanted to host a god.'

'She was a thirteen-year-old *child!*' Law bit off each word with venom.

'Who willingly followed her father. Her soul does not speak of coercion or betrayal. She went with the men her father said would be waiting for her. They worshipped her. She carried their god.'

'God? What *god*?' Law thought back to Camelia's diary, to her letters of pride and optimism.

A worm curling in her belly.

'Whatever came out of that girl was not a baby—mutated or otherwise,' Law said, swallowing painfully down his dry throat. 'You saw what I brought back the last time I was here. That umbilical cord didn't belong to a natural creature.'

'No, it did not,' Cait agreed.

'So what kind of *god* lays its eggs in little girls?'

The *cait sidhe* took a long, deep breath and closed her eyes. 'I don't know,' she admitted softly, as though the realisation pained her. 'As I said, her soul was damaged; fragments are missing. I can't see the whole picture. She was willing ... and then she was afraid—ashamed even. That's what drove her here. Away from her people. To die alone. At the hands of whatever she birthed.'

Law cast his mind back to the night he first found her—and the deformed foetus that attacked him. 'It tried to feed on me,' he mused aloud. 'Suckled at my neck like a baby vamp. Never heard of such a thing. Have you?'

Cait cast her eyes aside as she thought. 'No,' she said slowly. And then she stood, pushing up on her heels in a single, graceful movement. 'But I will confer with my people. It's time I went home. To the *aes sidhe*.'

'I broke your faerie ring.' His words were matter of fact, without remorse.

A half-smile quirked at Cait's lips. 'Whatever would I need that for?' Her eyes shone with their feline glow and she shrivelled down into a mound of fabric. A brief yowl, and Black Cat shot out from beneath the discarded dress and disappeared into the misty darkness of the Taschenwilde.

Law snorted. 'Fucking cats,' he muttered to himself and rose from his squat. The fire from the broken lantern was all but gone, and the shadows crept closer with unsettling malice. Law's arm throbbed terribly, as did his shoulder; he'd never dig a grave in this condition.

'Suppose I can't give you a proper burial after all,' he mumbled at the corpse.

Using the inner side of his boot, Law swept the leaves and fallen twigs away from Camelia's body, leaving a three-foot ring of exposed, wet earth around her. It was the best he could do—cremate her where she lay. He dragged the discarded trunk into the clearing, set the shovel aside, and took out the oil and salt. With a small, folded pocket blade hidden in the lining of the trunk, he pierced the hessian sack and let the small white crystals rain down on Camelia like snow. It probably wasn't necessary—the *cait sidhe* had eaten her corrupted soul. But if Law had learnt one thing from his work as an investigator, it was to never make assumptions. Protocol was protocol for a reason.

Lady Avery's ballgown lay discarded in the shadows. The hem of the skirt had turned black with mud and muck from the forest. Branches had torn a seam or two, but it was still far too fine a garment for a burial robe. Cleaned up and mended, it would probably fetch him some decent coin at the markets. It was enough to give him pause, especially since there was no truth to the little tale he'd spun Lady Avery about needing to wrap her in something from home to give her rest. But even in death, the departed deserved dignity—not to have their half-eaten corpse on display.

And so, Law draped the gown across the girl like a funeral shroud and doused it with the full bottle of oil. It took some searching to find a stick dry enough to catch alight in the dying lantern fire, but once it sparked, the makeshift pyre was ablaze in seconds. He took a step back, the flames burning hotter than he expected—hotter than *natural*. Averting his eyes from the intense brightness, Law turned towards the darkness of the forest, a sudden chill prickling across his skin.

Was the Taschenwilde... *helping him?* Lending him power from the ley line to ensure nothing but ash would remain?

He shivered again but paid it no further mind; whatever the reason, it suited his needs. Now there'd surely be no bones for a spirit to cling to, if any of it escaped the *cait sidhe's* gullet.

And every trace of that creature erased.

Law held a solemn vigil, alone in the Taschenwilde, for what seemed like hours. He cradled his bleeding arm across his chest as he watched the embers dance up into the sky and fizzle out. His head throbbed now the adrenaline of the ambush had fled his system; a tremor came into his fingers and chattered his teeth. The girl had died alone, and he still didn't know why. Had she finally woken up to the horror of her capture? Cait said she'd been worshipped, but perhaps she was scared in the end. Tried to run home and got lost.

'I suppose how you got here doesn't really matter,' Law muttered into the flames. Camelia Avery may have died alone, but he would see she had company as her bones reduced to ash. It gave him time to rehearse his report to Lady Avery. Should he tell her about her husband's role in Camelia's fate? If she read through the girl's journals when cleaning out her things, she'd likely piece it together on her own. Or would it be better she stayed ignorant? It wasn't easy for a woman to leave her husband, even among the well-to-do.

'Knowingly married to a monster or blissfully unaware—what's easier?' The latter, he supposed, and decided to tell Avery nothing further. Whatever cult Winston was involved with more than warranted an investigation, but it was too big an undertaking for just one man. Who knew how far the network spread or how sinister their operations were. He'd need to speak to Briar about that—after he'd been paid.

As the flames dwindled, and dawn rose over the Taschenwilde, Law smothered the remaining flames with damp earth and leaves. Thick white smoke billowed from the smouldering mound; Law coughed into his elbow as his eyes watered.

Camelia Avery was at peace, but the same uneasiness still rippled beneath Law's skin. What was it about this place? He looked at the scattered ghoul corpses and the remnants of the lantern fire. They'd made a real mess here, but no one was likely to care. People only entered the Taschenwilde to hide secrets, not unpack them. Law had tried that and failed.

With grey light slowly filling the forest, Law picked his way back through the densely packed trees towards Copperton and bed.

7

OMEN

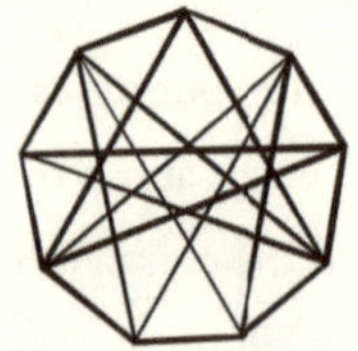

BRIAR WASN'T AT THE Dripping Bucket; Law frowned when the day manager told him as much. Briar Loren practically lived at the tavern, either in the kitchen or sequestered away in the wine cellar, brewing her tinctures and tonics. An oil lamp burned over her alchemy table, and a discarded pen had splattered tiny drops of ink across a page with a half-written sentence.

Law did not disturb the work—he knew better than to touch, smell or even *look* at whatever she was doing—and instead took the medicine chest off the shelf to his left. Kicking a stool out from under the laden table, he sat the chest atop it and cracked open the lid. His eyes burned at the wave of strong alcohol erupting from within. One of the glass phials was broken, a cork wedged in its fractured neck. Law picked it out with care and found some gauze to help pull the stopper free. The clear liquid was undoubtedly some sort of sterilant; he moistened the gauze and pressed it to his shredded arm. He hissed. It certainly stung like alcohol.

The ghoul's teeth had slashed deep into the meat, several of the punctures gaping open like red hungry mouths—they'd need stitches.

Wounds cleansed and dressed as best he could, Law left the wine cellar for the Chamberpots. He ached to his bones and needed sleep—Lady Avery would have to wait for her disappointing report. But as he rounded the corner onto the main cobbled throughfare, he saw smoke rising from the crest of the hill—Merigold Crescent.

Someone clipped Law's shoulder from behind and muttered a brisk apology as they raced past with a bucket, water sloshing onto the path. Law cursed and clenched his teeth; of *course* they'd collided with his injured shoulder.

Muttering obscenities under his breath, Law followed, his gait quickening to a jog. Half the town were headed to the Crescent, many with buckets and even more without. A fire in the affluent quarter reeked of scandal and everyone wanted a whiff of it.

Law knew it was the Avery estate even before it came into view. He pushed through the loitering crowd for a better vantage, eventually spying Lady Avery standing on the street before her burning house, handkerchief pressed to her nose and mouth.

She was not crying.

The fire was contained to the front turret, with water from the communal pump sprayed over the main homestead to keep it from catching. Smoke blackened the facade where flames lapped like thirsty tongues around the windows. A crash came from inside—falling beams? Toppled bookcases?—and then something burst through the closed panes of the upper level in a shower of shattered glass. It hit the ground with a dull thud. A gasp erupted from the crowd. Somebody screamed.

It wasn't Lady Avery.

She looked on, impassive, as two onlookers braved proximity to the flames to inspect the fallen body.

'Medic!' someone shouted, but it was futile. Blood poured from a wound to the head, a dark trail smearing across the ground as they pulled him away to safety. The neck lolled at a grotesque angle; if he hadn't died on impact, he was certainly dead now.

Law detached from the throng and took refuge under a tree alongside the house. The body belonged to Lord Winston Avery, a realisation that had dawned on the faces of those who'd tried to save him. They looked back to Lady Avery, heads shaking in disbelief and grief. With a stiff, solemn nod, she turned away, pausing as she spied Law beneath the tree. With all the casual grace of a woman on a leisurely stroll, she headed for him, face hard.

'What did you do?' Law asked quietly once she was in earshot. It was a sharp accusation to level at someone whose husband had just died, but he could tell by the rigidity of her spine that she held no remorse.

'I tidied up,' Lady Avery said, and looked back upon the carnage with a cool expression. 'Just like you said. I actually do feel better.'

'I said clear out Camelia's things, not burn down the fucking house. Why would you—' Law stopped abruptly when he realised. 'You read them.'

Law bit his tongue and waited instead for Avery to elaborate. The fire was more smoke than flame, now; the volunteers had mostly contained it in the tower, but the damage looked extensive. Lady Avery would need to find somewhere else to live.

Perhaps that's what she wanted.

'That monster corrupted my daughter,' she spat, venomous. 'Lured her into his sick cult until she was lost.' She looked at Law now, tears swelling her eyes. 'You should have seen the things she wrote in her journals. Sick, *twisted* things. Promises to offer herself to the church—to be a vessel for their desires. Is that what happened, then? What *he* let happen?' She stabbed a finger back in the direction of her husband's corpse.

'She tried to come back to you,' Law found himself saying. It wasn't a lie, but it might not be the truth, either. Camelia Avery had been on her way out of the Taschenwilde when she died; for all he knew, she *was* fleeing back to her mother. Yet her spirit had fought to keep them away from her writing desk—was she trying to hide her shame?

'She is at peace,' he offered. 'Try to find yours.'

'I already have,' she said. Simple. Hard.

He let that pass and joined her in watching the dying flames. He wanted to leave; already he had seen too many glares turn their way, hands cupped over mouths as they whispered scandalous stories to one another.

Law opened his mouth to excuse himself, but it was Lady Avery who spoke first.

'What happened to your arm?' she asked, eyebrow raised at the rough bandages around his right forearm. 'It stinks terribly.'

'Hazard of the job,' Law muttered, and then caught a whiff of the wound himself.

Shit.

'See that it gets proper attention. I'll send coin enough to have it treated and then some.' Her expression softened and she added, with warmth, 'You have my gratitude, Mr Reed. I would see you well enough to help others as you have helped me.'

Law bit back the instinct to correct her. To say he never helped her at all—Camelia was already dead. He didn't bring her back. Didn't bring justice to her killers. Lady Avery did that herself.

But he said nothing. Just ... closed his eyes and dipped his head, soaking it in. 'Send the coin to Briar Loren at The Dripping Bucket.' *Maybe she'll leave a bit for me.*

'Very well,' she said politely. 'Goodbye, Mr Reed. I wish you all the best in your recovery.'

LADY AVERY LEFT COPPERTON that evening. Took a carriage east to Harroveth, where she had a maternal cousin. It was the talk of the town the following day, when Law made his way to the Bucket to see Briar. He'd fallen into a deep sleep upon his return home, collapsing into bed at noon and not waking until late the next morning. The bright sun stung his eyes, raw and irritated from all the smoke. Haze hung low about the town, the air still fragrant with quenched flames. His arm throbbed to the bone; heavy, as if weighed down by a sack of bricks. The slightest touch sent pain burning through the limb all the way up to his shoulder. To even wiggle a finger was agony.

Briar Loren stood behind the bar of The Dripping Bucket, towelling out clean glassware to be placed back on the shelves. She glanced towards the door as the bell chimed Law's entrance, and he braced himself for a lashing from her sharp tongue. It never came. Not when he strode across the tavern and took a seat before her, nor when he raised his mangled arm to rest on the bar.

'Ghoul?' she asked, towel whipping around the lip of a pint glass.

'Ghoul,' Law confirmed grimly.

'Their bites fester rapidly.'

'So it would seem.'

Blood and fluid had seeped through the outermost bandages, staining the fabric a putrid yellow-brown. Briar's nose crinkled. Finally, she put the towel and glass aside and took out an ivory-handled pocket knife from her apron. It sawed through the gauze with stubborn persistence and Law exhaled as fresh air cooled his inflamed wounds.

'Elor's crooked finger, boy,' she growled.

'Can you fix it?'

'I can,' Briar confirmed, but her voice lacked the enthusiasm he was hoping for. 'But you'll be out of action for sometime.'

Law sighed; Briar took that as acquiescence. She grabbed one of the cleaned glasses, sat it down right side up and filled it with the good brandy from the top shelf. 'Get started while I collect some things from the wine cellar. We have better light here.'

Law saw to it that the brandy glass was empty by the time Briar returned with an assortment of medical paraphernalia. He recognised items from the kit he'd raided yesterday, along with phials of unknown tonics and dangerously sharp silver scalpels.

'I'll need more brandy before you start with those,' he said, dipping his head towards the blades. 'Whisky, preferably.'

Briar gave Law a hard stare. Whisky was for *paying* customers, and even those got theirs cut with water. She lifted a bottle from beneath the bar and took out another glass for herself.

'You're lucky your tab got cleared,' she said after knocking back her drink. 'Lady Avery was quite the generous client. She repaid your debt to me thrice over. Whatever will you do with all that coin?'

'Straight to the landlord.' Law gave a sardonic "*cheers*" to the air before downing his drink in a gulp. He grimaced as it burned its way down his gullet, but still shook the glass in Briar's direction, signalling for a refill.

'Back on the tab?' Briar asked mildly, obliging nonetheless.

Law sipped at it this time, relishing the distraction as the alchemist set to work on his wounds. She dabbed at him with all manner of pungent oils. Some stained his skin a bright golden yellow; others bubbled and stung the torn edges of flesh.

'You couldn't leave well enough alone,' she muttered, excising a ribbon of torn skin to neaten the wound for stitching. 'Had to go poking around the Taschenwilde. With *ghouls*, no less.'

Law groaned; he'd hoped to have been a few more drinks down before they had this conversation. 'You didn't see her, Briar.'

'I didn't have to.' The alchemist's words were a whisper—soft, like the way she blotted blood from his cuts. She fell silent, but Law knew her well enough to recognise she *wanted* to talk. With his free hand, he reached awkwardly into the breast pocket of his overcoat and pulled out the page of sketches from Camelia's diary.

The nine-sided star.

He slid it across the bar towards Briar. The alchemist glanced at it with hooded eyes.

'You've seen this before.' It wasn't a question.

Briar set the scalpel aside and poured another drink. 'Years ago, now,' she said, swallowing a mouthful. 'Before you came to town. Two children were found in the forest.' She started packing some sort of purple poultice into one of Law's open wounds; his lip curled back in a snarl at the pain before it cooled to a pleasant numbness. 'Two boys. Both young. One dead. Abdomen ripped open and empty. The surviving boy was so traumatised he didn't speak. We found no tracks nearby—nor a *foetus*, as you called it.' With a sad little laugh, she added, 'I thought we had werewolves. I sent an investigator to dig around, to try and find where the pack had holed up. But then, five days later, another body was found. At the old cathedral.' Her gaze was distant, looking past Law at the far wall, a wet sheen glossing them. 'It was my investigator—my protege, Ryce Rolland. He was ... bloody. His body puckered with punctures and pustules as if he'd been a feast for parasites. His eyes were missing. His tongue. And he was draped across the altar, in the centre of a nine-sided star painted in his own blood.'

It was Law's turn to reach for his whisky. He welcomed its burn this time. Hells, he'd welcome the bite of Briar's scalpel—anything to leach that image from his mind.

'What happened to the boy?'

Briar shook her head. 'I don't know. He'd followed Royce everywhere after he'd been rescued. But then...'

Law nodded as he digested the new information, watching as Briar sliced away bits of dead, shrivelled skin as if they weren't a part of his arm.

'We're dealing with a cult of some kind,' he offered. 'Humans who're messing with things they don't understand—or control.'

'Of course it's humans!' Briar spat. 'Not even vampyrs are that cruel. Which is why I *told* you to *leave it*. This is not our dominion. This is not for our people to die over. Let the Crown do something for a change.'

'They didn't get very far with Camelia's disappearance.'

Briar sighed, shoulders falling visibly. 'No. After all the effort I went to to get them here in the first place. Useless gilded bastards. I suspect their pockets are well lined. Probably with Winston's money.' Her fingertips were stained violet from the poultice; she wiped them on the dish cloth and started threading a wickedly curved needle.

Law tried not to look as Briar set about stitching the smaller wounds—the ones she hadn't packed with herbs and False Elor knew what. He didn't feel much, just an occasional tug, thanks to whatever anaesthetic she had used, but he knew once it wore off, he'd need more than a dram or two of whisky to douse it.

'I've been living with a *cait sidhe*,' Law offered the silence that filled the tavern.

'You didn't know?' Briar asked; Law sighed. Of course the ever astute Ms Loren would have figured it out.

'I let her eat Camelia Avery's soul,' he said.

'*Lawrence Henry Reed!*' the old woman chastised with alarm. The needle slipped in her dismay, driving so deep into his flesh he felt its sharp stab. He pulled away on instinct, flooding even more pain down his arm. With a growl, he settled—and reached for his whisky.

'She said she could give me answers,' Law admitted somewhat sheepishly. 'I wanted to have something to tell Lady Avery. *You* certainly could have been more forthcoming.'

Briar cooled at that. She refilled both their glasses; the bottle was already half-empty. 'Did you learn anything?'

'Nothing I hadn't gleaned from Camelia's diary,' Law admitted, ashamed. 'Her soul was too damaged. Something about it left her rattled. Said she needed to consult the *aes sidhe*.'

'False Elor, the last thing we need is faeries interfering in things,' Briar cursed. Tenderly, she lifted Law's wrist and passed a strip of gauze beneath it. She wrapped it firm and gentle, like swaddling a babe. When finished, she cupped her gnarled hand atop the bandages and watched Law wordlessly for a moment.

'No more ghouls for a while,' she insisted. 'No more *anything*. Those wounds go sour fast. No over-exertion. Keep your body strong.'

Law scoffed and reached into his jacket for his cigarillo case. He placed one between his lips and fumbled with his tinderbox. It dropped from his hand, but Briar caught it and held it to the stick until it caught. Law drew a long drag, closing his eyes as the smoke filled his lungs.

'What am I supposed to do until then?' he mumbled around the cigarillo.

Briar shrugged. 'Samhain's just around the corner. Be plenty of interesting folks in town for that. Tumblers, bards. An exotic dancer or two.'

Law choked on his smoke and started coughing. 'When have you ever seen me interested in *exotic dancers*?'

She shrugged again. 'First time for everything, Mr Reed. First time for everything.'

He grunted and fell back into silence. His stomach rumbled, somewhere underneath the swirl of liquor. It would be close to noon now; soon, the Bucket's first patrons would roll in the doors and fill the seats until nightfall.

'And what about this cult?' he asked, pushing out another cloud of smoke. 'Still think it's not our business?'

Briar avoided answering by tightening the cork on the whisky bottle and returning it below the bar. She chose her words more carefully than usual, avoiding Law's probing gaze as she considered how best to respond. 'I suppose we can't ignore it, no.' Quickly, she added, 'But nor do we chase it, understand? We see that symbol again, we record it. Do what we can to find answers. But that's it. We do not go digging.'

'You don't want justice for Ryce Rolland?' Law asked and he saw Briar's jaw harden.

'Of course I do, Mr Reed,' she seethed. 'But I know to pick my battles. And it's certainly not with a pack of ghouls in the Taschenwilde.'

Law chuckled dryly as she flicked him with her dishtowel. He stubbed out his crinkled cigarillo and swivelled around on his stool, looking out over the emptiness of the daytime tavern. Drops of his blood had splashed on the ground during Briar's enthusiastic cleansing of his wounds. He stretched out his leg and swept sawdust over the red droplets until they were just another stain on the floor.

Whatever happened to that boy, Law wondered, watching the nervous blond bard set up in the back corner of the tavern. He'd picked a rough time to start a new residency, with the town about to be inundated with talented entertainers for the end of harvest festivities. If he was smart, he'd pack up and leave with a travelling troupe.

Get out of here while you can! He wanted to shout like an unimpressed heckler. But he didn't. Instead, he called for another drink and nursed his bandaged arm in his lap, admiring the neatness of Briar's dressing. At least *he* didn't have to wait for Samhain for things to be interesting around here.

There are more adventures to be had in Dallalmar ...

Coming soon.

Did You Enjoy This Book?

If you enjoyed **Parasitic Omens**, please consider leaving a review.

As an indie author, reviews are essential in getting the story into the hands of more likeminded readers.

So whether you share it to your socials, recommend it to a friend or leave a simple, one sentence review, know that every little bit helps.

See you in the next installment!

ACKNOWLEDGEMENTS

Dear Reader,

Thank you for joining me on another adventure—or perhaps your first.

Having spent the best part of my life immersed in the creation of *Gardens of War & Wasteland* it was as terrifying as it was exciting bringing a new world to life. As such, this project has been 12 months in the making—and it's only just getting started!

I hope you've enjoyed your first trip to Dallalmar. I assure you there are many more adventures to be had with Law and the supernatural. But first I must thank the team who made this book happen, especially when it felt like I'd never finish anything of worth again.

Krystle, Connor, Fiona and the rest of the Discord group: thank you for enduring my endless moaning and despair. Without your support and encouragement I quite literally would not have gotten through the dreaded Second Book Blues. You're always there to give me perspective, compassion and most importantly, love. Thank you. So very, very much.

To Anna Stephens, my editor, mentor and inspiration: your ruthless red pen has been instrumental in helping this story not only be the best that it could, but served to solidify the foundation of a longer series to come.

My family: thank you for keeping my head above water. Without you, I would drown.

And finally, you, dear reader. Whether this is your first book or your fifth, thank you for being here.

I hope you'll stay.

xx

jam

PS – read on to enjoy a sneak peek at Chapter One of **The Ruptured Sky** ...

CHARACTER ART

LAWRENCE
REED

BRIAR LOREN

CAIT
SIDHE

THE RUPTURED SKY

SNEAK PEEK

CHAPTER ONE
AMIKHARLIA

THERE WAS BLOOD UNDER her fingernails.

Amika ran her knife along the ukarat's gut and began to peel back the skin. The kill had been clean: pierced through the skull, the demonspawn's short, bristly pelt was in pristine condition and would fetch her a handsome price. Kneeling among the long grass of the plain under the shroud of a starless night, she worked carefully to remove the spinal barbs along with the fur. When it was fully detached from the corpse, Amika rolled the pelt into a ball and tucked it into a blotchy old satchel; demon blood stained as well as ink.

There was just one thing left to do. Amika drew her sword. Castle-forged and inlaid with gold and sapphire, it was her pride and joy—and the one piece of her past she allowed herself to carry. With a brief flourish, she brought the blade down on the beast's neck, severing head from body. From her belt she pulled a butcher's meat hook and pierced the ukarat's eye socket.

Heaving her trophy over her shoulder, Amika headed back towards the capital.

THYNOR'S TANNERY STANK TO the realm adjacent. It lay far from the busy taverns and market stalls, nestled in a decrepit residential block long abandoned by its old imperial inhabitants. A bell chimed upon Amika's entry. Thynor, a stocky Qhoraakese man with a shiny bald head and forearms thicker than her thighs, hummed joyously as he scraped the decaying hair from a previously cured cowhide. The tanner was seemingly impervious to the reek of shit, piss and rot that filled the high-ceilinged room; Amika had to breathe through her mouth.

'Kharli, my sweet! Right on time.' Thynor beamed, teeth bright against skin the same mahogany shade as Amika's hair.

'Do I ever let you down?'

'Nay, never.' Wiping his hands on his viscera-stained apron, Thynor approached. 'What have yer brought me today, my sweet?'

Amika swung the meat hook and the ukarat head hit the bench with a muted *thud*. Thynor let out a delighted rumble from the depth of his throat. He picked up the head, eagerly examining the prize. A meaty tongue flopped out of the ukarat's slack jowls, angled around the finger-long teeth of its jaw.

'Look at that,' he said, brushing his thumb over the neat puncture just below the horn on the demonspawn's forehead. 'Such precision! The accuracy of yer blade is astounding. I trust the skin is just as perfect?'

Confidence brought a smile to Amika's face as she unrolled the ukarat pelt across the bench. 'Just as perfect.'

Thynor chuckled again. 'Yer've outdone yerself, my sweet. Look at that. Even the barbs are intact. A perfect throw rug, this is. Sure yer don't want it for yer room?'

'I'll pass, thanks. Sell it to a mercenary. Let them decorate their guild halls with lies.'

The tanner set his palms down flat on the bench, eyes turning serious. 'I'll give yer five bronze fer it.'

'Five *bronze?* The head alone is worth a silver!'

Laughter erupted like water from a burst dam. '*Ha!* The look on yer face! I kid, my sweet, I kid. Ten gold, as always. I'll even throw in three silvers fer messin' with yer.'

'Well, you can direct that to Lomi,' Amika said. 'My board is due at month's end.'

Thynor nodded as he packed up his purchases and sat them on a pile of other pelts ready to cure. 'And how is Lominah Deen?' he asked, returning to the front bench. 'Cooking up a storm, no doubt, with the Flame Moon just around the corner. What do you Meytarans call it—the Fall Festival?'

Amika frowned. 'Festival of the Fall,' she corrected. 'And it's hardly the same thing. You pay homage to your Deity while we remember the collapse of an empire.'

'Aye, aye. Busy time in Ciraselo regardless. Got a whole bunch o' leather ready for the night markets. Plan on making a killin' this year.'

'You do every year, Thyne.' Amika slung her empty satchel over her shoulder and made for the door. 'I'll keep an eye on the mark board for any more rikkara sightings. Might actually let you keep the leather this time.'

'Aye, you do that, my sweet.' The tanner waved a meaty hand. 'Give my best to Lomi.'

Amika headed towards the tavern she called home, stomach rumbling after talk of Lomi's cooking. It was a long walk through the old capital, made longer by the ache in her limbs and the fuzziness in her head. She always felt ill after a hunt. Not from the brutality or the gore, but from the process itself, the exhaustion that took hold with every demonspawn skull she speared. It was good money—easy money, in some ways—and no matter how dirty it seemed, it was the life she'd chosen. She wished she could stop the blood getting under her fingernails, though.

LOMINAH DEEN'S TAVERN WAS nestled in the heart of Spicers' Alley, the row of market stalls dealing purely in dried produce and gemstones from the west. Amika had been renting a room above the bar for the last four years, ever since she'd helped Lomi's then-heavily pregnant daughter Nylah carry some ale barrels. The Deens had been kind to her, a young woman of a foolish eighteen years who was so very far from home, and had given her shelter and purpose. It hadn't taken long for her to think of them as family.

'Yer better get yerself cleaned up before yer even *think* about putting yer arse in that chair,' Lominah said by way of greeting the moment Amika passed through the door. 'And don't yer be traipsing that inky muck through my nice clean bar, either.'

'Come now, Lomi, I'm not that bad!' Amika smiled, gesturing to her blood-splattered tunic.

Lomi, who held a cleaning rag in one hand while she pulled ale with the other, rolled her eyes. The Qhoraakese woman was always busy, and she was happier for it. A warm smile parted her lips and her long wave of black curls seemed to dance along with the jovial sway of her body.

'Aye, there are more foul types than you in 'ere, girl. Come, sit. What'll yer have?'

Amika slipped into a stool. 'What happened to the window?' She pointed at a set of broken shutters on the storefront.

Lominah sighed. 'Another freak windstorm. Was airing the stink outta this place when a gale came from nowhere and blew my damn shutters in. I'll get around to fixing it one day.'

A roving waiter strode from the kitchen, his tray laden with mounds of freshly carved meat, rich with spice and gravy. Lominah waved him over and started piling various cuts onto a plate for Amika.

'Thynor's pleased with the bounty,' Amika said, salivating at the sight of the food. She bent over the bar to pour her own ale. 'Paid me a bonus.'

'Don't take much to please Thynor.' Lomi pushed the meaty feast towards Amika and slid a fold of parchment alongside it. Glancing around briefly, she leant in close. 'This came for yer.'

Amika eyed the note with a furrowed brow. It was unsealed, unmarked by any distinguishing insignias—the third of its kind to arrive this month. She snatched it off the bench and crumpled it inside her tunic. 'I thought he would've given up by now,' she muttered.

'Redda's not one to be ignored,' Lomi said darkly. 'Heard him and his crew are onto something ... *strange*. Might be worth hearing him out.'

Amika grunted. She took a big mouthful of roasted meat, savouring the way the fire pepper tingled her tongue. There was enough *strange* in her life already—she didn't need some lowlife mercenary adding to it.

'Aunty Kharli!'

Amika turned to see a little boy bounding down the stairs towards her. His eyes were big and dark, his hair as curled and bouncy as Lominah's.

'Zozo!' Amika beamed as he leapt into her arms. 'What are you doing here? Where's your mother?'

'Gone east to see the shipment to Cirahk,' Lomi said. She ruffled the boy's hair. 'Zorel's staying with his grandmama 'til she's back.'

'And I bet she's excited to have you all to herself!'

'Aye, so long as he stays outta the kitchens and doesn't bother the customers, it's a pleasure to have him. My only grandbaby, after all.'

Amika lifted the little boy and sat him on the edge of the bar. He was the spitting image of Nylah, and she couldn't help but smile at the reminder of her friend. They hadn't seen each other much lately, since Nylah had remarried and given up working at the bar to open a gem emporium with her new husband. The store wasn't too far from Spicers' Alley, but with Amika's hunting and Nylah's fledgling business, it was difficult to catch a meal together.

'I've gotten real good at hiding, Aunty Kharli!' Zorel said, flashing his crooked smile. With a whisper he added, 'No one's been able to find me yet.'

'Sounds like I've got a challenge on my hands.' Amika grinned and tickled his belly. Raucous laughter filled the tavern and Zorel almost wiggled himself right off the bar.

'Enough of that now,' Lomi grumbled. 'Why don't yer go hide yerself up in yer room?' She placed her grandson back on his feet and sent him running upstairs with a playful tap on his backside. 'And you,' she added, turning back to Amika, 'don't leave Redda hanging.

Don't want none of his grunts barging in 'ere with knives. Yer got it, girl?'

'I promise, Lomi.'

'Good. Yer know I don't run that kinda joint,' she said, just as a drunk went crashing through a table.

'I ONCE KILLED A man while he was takin' a piss,' Redda said, dagger tumbling casually across his knuckles. 'Knifed 'im right in the neck.'

The enormous man grinned across the table, half-lit by the wax candle that melted between Amika and himself. He had a booming voice, hair like a bear's hide and a scar down the right side of his one-eyed face. Around them, the air was thick with the bouquet of floral-sweet Kheshtarli ale that lined the walls in oaken barrels. The bar where Redda had insisted they meet was full of drunken southerners clinking glasses and sloshing ale onto the stone-tiled floor. Despite the crowds, they gave Amika's table a wide berth.

'Is that supposed to impress me?' Amika said, spearing an apple with the tip of her knife. Sliding it free with her other hand, she set to peeling back the red skin. 'I hunt beasts, not men.'

Redda's eye drifted to the boiled leather jerkin she wore over her tunic, armour crafted from the hide of a rikkara, a boar-like demon-spawn from the realm adjacent. The beast was a rare quarry, far more valuable than the common ukarat; Amika sported the garment as a trophy.

'Aye, a good sword arm on yer, that's fer sure. Girl like you could go far in this world. Right guild, right commander. Aye, girl like you could go far.'

'What do you want, Redda?' Amika pressed, eyes narrowing. He had only summoned her to neutral ground in the Kheshtarli tavern for one reason: to pitch an offer. But it would not work. She had no interest in joining the Talons. Kharli the Demon Huntress worked alone.

The Commander of the Talons chuckled into his pint. 'Sharp as a Kheshtarli blade, aren't yer? Aye, I do want somethin'.' Redda slipped a hand inside his sweat-stained tunic and tossed a hessian sack onto the table. 'I'm sure yer'll want it too.'

Amika crunched a sliver of apple as she eyed what looked like a spicer's bag of herbs. Brows knitted, she raised her gaze to Redda. With a crooked smile, the commander reached into the sack. Nestled in his palm were a number of frozen crystals, shimmering azure. Looking closer, Amika saw a flicker beneath the glasslike surface. And then she felt it—the familiar itching under her skin; the marching of thousands of ants through her veins.

Amika shivered and leant away.

Redda's grin widened. He picked out one of the crystals and slid the others back into the bag. Holding it between his thumb and index finger, the gnarled commander studied the shining gem.

'Those Yaians in the north,' he continued, 'they used to pass 'em out to the Skrevaari. Tokens o' esteem, they called them. Thanks for havin' let 'em invade the northerners' land. And the Skrevaari, well, they traded 'em wide 'n far, didn't they? Thought they was nought but pretty stones.'

'So what are they?' Amika kept her face passive. She was not one to be charmed by fables from the ruins of Skrevaar, but her gaze was fixed on the crystal in the commander's hand. It exuded a soft blue glow in contrast to the red hues of the tavern lighting. Its ethereal pulse continued to torment the itch under her skin, growing stronger the longer she stared.

'Tears of Yaia—Skrevaari magic stones. Vessels for the demon-power that brought down the empire.' A raspy laugh rumbled from Redda's throat. 'Crush the stones and—'

He encased the crystal in his fist and it shattered. Between them, the candlewick flared, spewing blue-hot flames up to the ceiling. Shock echoed around the tavern. Dice rolls paused and dozens of eyes turned to them.

Amika gripped the edge of the table, knuckles white. As the fire died, so did the interest of the drunken patrons. They soon returned to their games and drink.

Amika leant closer. 'Why are you showing me this?'

Redda moved in to meet her. 'Because I be needin' yer help.'

'For what?' She kept her jaw clenched; her insides were a quivering mess. Did he know of the secret scratching beneath her flesh?

Redda's eye flicked back to the unassuming bag. 'Not many of these 'ere stones left in the world. Fetch a mighty price, they do.' He reclined in his chair. 'Now, Kharli, yer not one of the power players in this 'ere city, but a bit o' gold is never spat upon. These puny pebbles 'ere don't pack much in power and are worth less than a barrel of ale, but me sources say more ... *potent* ones exist. In Li'Nea Wood.' His lopsided grin grew as his lips formed the words.

Li'Nea Wood. The dark, dense thicket to the east. The common-folk were all well-versed in tales from the Wood—tales of an ageless man with eyes as black as demon blood and a soul to match. Get too close to the forest's edge and risk falling prey to his venom—a toxic miasma that bred illness not unlike the Sickness, which tore through old Mey and sent their ancestors fleeing across the Azure Expanse. Who ever started that ridiculous story certainly knew what they were doing. Fear of the devastating bloodplague hung over the people still; any unexplained lurgy sent the populace running for the safety of closed doors faster than a hot summer's wind across the Plains.

'You want me to slay the ukarats so you can chase some old man from a folktale?' Amika surmised.

The commander's laugh bellowed once more. 'Sharp indeed! Aye, I want yer to help me boys with the demonspawn. This warlock in the Wood—if anyone in the realm has the crystals, it'll be 'im.'

Amika traced a fingertip around the rim of her half-drunk ale. 'What's in it for me?'

'A cut o' the bounty, o' course. Consider these a gesture o' good will.' He nudged the sack of gems towards her.

It was a decent offer. If these Tears of Yaia were as rare and coveted as Redda claimed, their sale would pay the board on her dingy tavern room until spring. But it took more than the promise of gold to sway her interest.

The little hessian parcel pulled Amika's gaze once again. Could this be the sign she was searching for? The path that would lead her to answers?

Her resolve strengthened as she curled her fingers around the ale tankard and held it high. 'To business,' she said, tipping her head towards Redda.

'To business,' the commander echoed.

The deal was sealed with a *clink*.

The story continues in *The Ruptured Sky: Gardens of War & Waste-land Book I.*

Available now.

NEWSLETTER JAM

Sign up for **Jessica A. McMinn**'s mailing list to receive exclusive insights and updates from her #writerslife, including two FREE **Gardens of War & Wasteland** novellas, **The Collector's Lost Things** and **Call of the Huntress**.

About Author

 Jessica A. McMinn is a speculative fiction author based in regional NSW, Australia, with a passion for dark fantasy, coffee and cats.

Since graduating from the University of Wollongong with Distinction in BCA (Creative Writing) and BA (Japanese), Jessica has spent five years in Japan teaching English and refining her craft. She now works as a freelance writer.

When she is not writing, Jessica enjoys playing video games, drawing, crafting and raising her two beautiful children while constantly pleading for the cat not to piss on the carpet.

For art prints, merchandise and more, check out the JAMstore